A wicked smile broke out across her face as she downed the entire drink. A stray droplet escaped the co⬚⬚⬚⬚ f her mouth and Chant⬚⬚⬚ ⬚⬚⬚⬚⬚ her tongue. Goc⬚

'It's the *champa*⬚⬚⬚⬚⬚⬚⬚⬚⬚⬚⬚⬚⬚⬚

'Well, if you keep⬚⬚⬚⬚⬚⬚⬚⬚⬚⬚⬚…'

'I might get my⬚⬚ ⬚⬚to trouble.' She pulled a serious face, her cheeks flushed with the alcohol.

She'd looked like this the night he'd danced with her at Weeping Reef. Chantal had always been the serious type—studious and sensible until she'd had a drink or two. Then the hardness seemed to melt away, she loosened up, and the playful side came out. If she'd been tempting before, she was damn near impossible to resist now.

'You always seem to treat trouble like it's a bad idea.' Brodie divested her of her champagne flute before tugging her to him.

'Isn't that the definition of trouble?' Her hands hovered at his chest, barely touching him.

He shouldn't be pulling her strings the way he did when he wanted a girl. He liked to wind them up first. Tease them…get them to laugh. Relax their boundaries. He was treating Chantal as if he wanted to sleep with her…and he did.

He ⬚⬚⬚⬚⬚⬚⬚⬚⬚⬚⬚⬚⬚⬚⬚⬚⬚⬚⬚⬚⬚⬚⬚⬚⬚⬚ t stop him⬚

'Ba⬚

SWANSEA LIBRARIES

6000230921

SYDNEY'S MOST ELIGIBLE...

The men everyone *is talking about!*

Young, rich and gorgeous, Rob, Scott, Brodie
and Luke have the world at their feet
and women queuing to get between their sheets.

Find out how the past and the present collide for them in
this stylish, sexy and glamorous new quartet!

These sexy Sydney tycoons didn't get to the top by taking
the easy way—the only thing they love more than a
challenge is a woman who knows her mind!

So let the fireworks begin…!

HER BOSS BY DAY…
by Joss Wood
Available January 2015

THE MILLIONAIRE'S PROPOSITION
by Avril Tremayne
Available February 2015

THE TYCOON'S STOWAWAY
by Stefanie London
Available March 2015

THE HOTEL MAGNATE'S DEMAND
by Jennifer Rae
Available April 2015

You won't want to miss any of the fabulous books
in this sizzling mini-series!

THE TYCOON'S STOWAWAY

BY
STEFANIE LONDON

All rights reserved including the right of reproduction in whole
or in part in any form. This edition is published by arrangement with
Harlequin Books S.A.

This is a work of fiction. Names, characters, places, locations and
incidents are purely fictional and bear no relationship to any real
life individuals, living or dead, or to any actual places, business
establishments, locations, events or incidents. Any resemblance is
entirely coincidental.

This book is sold subject to the condition that it shall not, by way of
trade or otherwise, be lent, resold, hired out or otherwise circulated
without the prior consent of the publisher in any form of binding or
cover other than that in which it is published and without a similar
condition including this condition being imposed on the subsequent
purchaser.

® and TM are trademarks owned and used by the trademark owner
and/or its licensee. Trademarks marked with ® are registered with the
United Kingdom Patent Office and/or the Office for Harmonisation in
the Internal Market and in other countries.

Published in Great Britain 2015
by Mills & Boon, an imprint of Harlequin (UK) Limited,
Eton House, 18-24 Paradise Road, Richmond, Surrey, TW9 1SR

© 2015 Harlequin S.A.

Special thanks and acknowledgement are given to Stefanie London
for her contribution to the *Sydney's Most Eligible...* series.

ISBN: 978-0-263-24852-4

Harlequin (UK) Limited's policy is to use papers that are natural,
renewable and recyclable products and made from wood grown in
sustainable forests. The logging and manufacturing processes conform
to the legal environmental regulations of the country of origin.

Printed and bound in Spain
by CPI, Barcelona

Stefanie London lives in Melbourne with her very own hero and enough books to sink a ship. She frequently indulges in her passions for good coffee, French perfume, high heels and zombie movies. During the day she uses lots of words like *synergy* and *strategy*. At night she writes sexy contemporary romance stories and tries not to spend too much time shopping online and watching baby animal videos on YouTube.

Books by Stefanie London

Breaking the Bro Code
Only the Brave Try Ballet

**Visit the author profile page at
www.millsandboon.co.uk for more titles**

CITY AND COUNTY OF SWANSEA LIBRARIES	
6000230921	
Askews & Holts	12-Mar-2015
	£3.99
HQ	

To my wonderful husband for supporting me from the very first time I wrote 'Chapter One'. Thank you for always understanding my need to write, for keeping me sane through the ups and downs, and for holding my hand when I took the biggest leap of my life.

I love you.

Always.

PROLOGUE

HOT. LOUD. CRUSHING.

The dance floor at the Weeping Reef resort bar was the perfect way to shake off the work day, and for Chantal Turner it was the perfect place to practise her moves. She swung her hips to the pulsating beat of the music, her hands raking through her hair and pushing damp strands from her forehead. A drop of perspiration ran in a rivulet down her back but she wouldn't stop. At midnight, the night was still in its infancy, and she would dance until her feet gave out.

She was enjoying a brief interlude away from her life plan in order to soak up the rays while earning a little money in the glorious Whitsundays. But the second she was done she'd be back on the mainland, working her butt off to secure a place at a contemporary dance company. She smiled to herself. The life in front of her was bright and brimming with opportunity.

Tonight the majority of her crew hadn't come out. Since Chantal's boyfriend wasn't much of a dancer he stood at the bar, sipping a drink and chatting to another resort employee. No matter—the music's beat flowing through her body was the only companion she needed. Her black dress clung to damp skin. The holiday crowd had peaked for the season, which meant the dance floor was even more densely packed than usual.

'Pretty girls shouldn't have to dance on their own.'

A low, masculine voice rumbled close to her ear and the scent of ocean spray and coconut surfboard wax hit her nostrils, sending a shot of heat down to her belly.

She would know that smell anywhere. A hand rested lightly on her hip, but she didn't cease the gentle rolling of her pelvis until the beat slowed down.

'Don't waste your pick-up lines on me, Brodie.' She turned and stepped out of his grip. 'There are plenty of other ladies in holiday mode who would appreciate your cheesy come-ons.'

'Cheesy?' He pressed a hand against his well-muscled chest. 'You're a harsh woman, Chantal.'

The tanned expanse of his shoulders stretched out from under a loose-fitting black tank top, a tattoo peeking out at the neckline. Another tattoo of an anchor stretched down his inner forearm. He stared at her, shaggy sun-bleached hair falling around his lady-killer face and light green eyes.

He's off-limits, Chantal. Super off-limits. Don't touch him...don't even think *about it.*

Brodie Mitchell stepped forward to avoid the flailing arms of another dancer, who'd apparently indulged in a few too many of the resort's signature cocktails. He bumped his hip against hers, and their arms brushed as Chantal continued to dance. She wasn't going to let Brodie and his amazing body prevent her from having a good time.

The song changed and she thrust her hands into the air, swinging her hips again, bumping Brodie gently. His fingertips gripped her hips like a magnet had forced them together. Every touch caused awareness to surge through her veins.

'You can't dance like that and expect me not to join in.'

His breath was hot against her ear. Her whole body tingled as the effects of the cocktails she'd downed before hitting the dance floor descended. The alcohol warmed her, giving her limbs a languid fluidity. Head spinning, she tried to step out of his grip, but stumbled when another dancer knocked into her. She landed hard up against Brodie, her hands flat against his rock-hard chest. He smelled good. So. *Damn*. Good.

Against her better judgment she ran her palms up and down his chest, swinging her hips and rolling her head back. The music flowed through her, its heavy bass thundering in her chest. She probably shouldn't have had so many Blue Hawaiians—all that rum and blue curaçao had made her head fuzzy.

'I can dance however I like,' she said, tilting her chin up at him defiantly. 'Mr Cheese.'

'You're going to pay for that.' He grinned, snaking his arm around her waist and drawing her even closer. 'There's a difference between charming and cheesy, you know.'

'You think you're *charming*?' she teased, ignoring the building tension that caused her centre to throb mercilessly. It was the alcohol—it always made her horny. It was absolutely *nothing* to do with Brodie.

'I do happen to think I'm charming.'

His lips brushed against her ear, and each bump of his thighs sent shivers down her spine.

'I've had it confirmed on a number of occasions too.'

'How *many* women have confirmed it?' She bit back a grin, curious as to the number of notches on his bedpost. Brodie had a bit of a reputation and, as much as she hated to admit it, Chantal could see why.

It wasn't just that he had a gorgeous face and a body that looked as if it belonged in a men's underwear commercial. Hot guys were a dime a dozen at the resort. Brodie had something extra: a cheeky sense of humour coupled with the innate ability to make people feel comfortable around him. He had people eating out of the palm of his hand.

'I don't kiss and tell.'

'Come on—I'll even let you round up to the nearest hundred.' She pulled back to look him in the eye while she traced a cross over her heart with one finger.

He grabbed her wrist and pulled her hand behind his back, forcing her face close to his. 'I'm not as bad as you think, Little Miss Perfect.'

'I doubt that very much.'

The music switched to a slow, dirty grind and Brodie nudged his thigh between hers. A gasp escaped her lips as her body fused to his. She should stop now. This was *so wrong*. But it felt better than anything else could have right at that moment. Better than chocolate martinis and Sunday sleep-ins...even better than dancing on a stage. A hum of pleasure reverberated in her throat.

'I bet you're even worse.'

'Ha!' His hand came up to cup the side of her jaw. 'You want to know for sure, don't you?'

Her body cried out in agreement, her breath hitching as his face hovered close to hers. The sweet smell of rum on his lips mingled with earthy maleness, hitting her with a force powerful enough to make her knees buckle.

Realisation slammed into her, her jaw dropping as she jerked backwards. His eyes reflected the same shock. Reality dawned on them both. This was more than a little harmless teasing—in fact it didn't feel harmless at all.

How could she possibly have fallen for Brodie? He was a slacker—an idle charmer who talked his way through life instead of working hard to get what he wanted. He was her opposite—a guy so totally wrong for her it was almost comical. Yet the feel of his hands on her face, the bump of his pelvis against hers, and the whisper of his breath at her cheek was the most intoxicating thing she'd ever experienced.

Oh, no! This is not happening... This is not *happening.*

'You feel it, don't you?' Worry streaked across his face

and his hands released her as quickly as if he'd touched a boiling pot. 'Don't lie to me, Chantal.'

'I—'

Her response was cut short when something flashed at the corner of her eye. *Scott.*

'What the *hell* is going on?' he roared. His cheeks were flushed scarlet, his mouth set into a grim line.

'It's nothing, man.' Brodie held up his hands in surrender and stepped back.

He was bigger than Scott, but he wasn't a fighter. The guilt in his eyes mirrored that in Chantal's heart. How could she have done this? How could she have fallen for her boyfriend's best friend?

'Didn't look like nothing to me. You had your hands all over her!'

'It's nothing, Scott,' Chantal said, grabbing his arm. But he shook her off. 'We were just dancing.'

'Ha!' The laugh was a sharp stab of a sound—a laugh without a hint of humour. 'Tell me you don't feel anything for Brodie. Because it sure as hell didn't look like a platonic dance between friends.'

She tried to find the words to explain how she felt, but she couldn't. She closed her eyes and pressed her palm to her forehead. She opened them in time to see Scott's fist flying at Brodie's face.

'No!'

CHAPTER ONE

REJECTION WAS HARD ENOUGH for the average person, and for a dancer it was constant. The half-hearted 'Thanks, but no thanks' after an unsuccessful audition? Yep, she'd had those. Bad write-up from the arts section of a local paper? Inevitable. An unenthusiastic audience? Unpleasant, but there'd be at least one in every dancer's career.

Chantal Turner had been told it got easier, but it didn't feel easy now to keep her chin in the air and her lips from trembling. Standing in the middle of the stage, with spotlights glaring down at her, she shifted from one bare foot to the other. The faded velvet of the theatre seats looked like a sea of red in front of her, while the stage lights caused spots to dance in her vision.

The stage was her favourite place in the whole world, but today it felt like a visual representation of her failure.

'I'm afraid your style is not quite what we're looking for,' the director said, toying with his phone. 'It's very...'

He looked at his partner and they both shook their heads.

'Traditional,' he offered with a gentle smile. 'We're looking for dancers with a more modern, gritty style for this show.'

Chantal contemplated arguing—telling him that she could learn, she could adapt her style. But the thought of them saying no all over again was too much to deal with.

'Thanks, anyway.'

At least she'd been allocated the last solo spot for the day, so no one was left to witness her rejection. She stopped for a moment to scuff her feet into a pair of sneakers and throw a hoodie over her tank top and shorts.

The last place had told her she was too abstract. Now she was too traditional. She bit down on her lower lip to keep the protest from spilling out. Some feedback was better than none, no matter how infuriatingly contradictory it was. Besides, it wasn't professional to argue with directors—and she was, if nothing else, a professional. A professional who couldn't seem to book any decent jobs of late...

This was the fourth audition she'd flunked in a month. Not even a glimmer of interest. They'd watched her with poker faces, their feedback delivered with surgical efficiency. The reasons had varied, but the results were the same. She knew her dancing was better than that.

At least it had used to be...

Her sneakers crunched on the gravel of the theatre car park as she walked to her beat-up old car. She was lucky the damn thing still ran; it had rust spots, and the red paint had flaked all over the place. It was so old it had a cassette player, and the gearbox *always* stuck in second gear. But it was probably the most reliable thing in her life, since all the time she'd invested in her dance study didn't seem to be paying off. Not to mention her bank accounts were looking frighteningly lean.

No doubt her ex-husband, Derek, would be pleased to know that.

Ugh—she was *not* going to think about that stuffy control freak, or the shambles that had been her marriage.

Sliding into the driver's seat, she checked her phone. A text from her mother wished her luck for her audition. She cringed; this was just another opportunity to prove she'd wasted all the sacrifices her mother had made for her dancing.

Staring at herself in the rearview mirror, Chantal pursed her lips. She would *not* let this beat her. It was a setback, but only a minor one. She'd been told she was a gifted dancer on many occasions. Hell, she'd even been filmed for a documentary on contemporary dance a few years back. She *would* get into one of these companies, even if it took every last ounce of her resolve.

Despite the positive affirmation, doubt crept through her, winding its way around her heart and lungs and stomach. Why was everything going so wrong now?

Panic rose in her chest, the bubble of anxiety swelling and making it hard to breathe. She closed her eyes and forced a long breath, calming herself. Panicking would not help. Thankfully, she'd finally managed to book a short-term dancing job in a small establishment just outside of Sydney. It wasn't prestigious. But it didn't have to be forever.

A small job would give her enough money to get herself through the next few weeks—*and* there was accommodation on site. She *would* fix this situation. No matter what.

She clenched and unclenched her fists—a technique she'd learned once to help relax her muscles whenever panic swelled. It had become a technique she relied on more and more. Thankfully the panic attacks were less like tidal waves these days, and more like the slosh of a pool after someone had dive-bombed. It wasn't ideal, but she could manage it.

Baby steps... Every little bit of progress counts.

Shoving the dark thoughts aside, she pulled out of the car park and put her phone into the holder stuck to the window. As if on cue the phone buzzed to life with the smiling face of her old friend Willa. Chantal paused before answering. She wasn't in the mood to talk, but she had a two-hour drive to get to her gig and music would only keep her amused for so long.

Besides, since her divorce Chantal had realised that real friends were few and far between, so she'd been making more of an effort to keep in touch with Willa. Ignoring her call now would go completely against that.

She tapped the screen of her phone and summoned her most cheerful voice. 'Hey, Willa.'

'How's our favourite dancer?'

Willa's bubbly greeting made a wave of nostalgia wash over her.

'Taking the arts world by storm, I hope?'

Chantal forced a laugh. 'Yeah, something like that. It's a slow process, but I'm working on it.'

'You'll get there. I know it. That time I saw you dance at the Sydney Opera House was incredible. We're all so proud of you for following your dream.'

Chantal's stomach rocked. She knew not everyone Willa referred to would be proud of her—especially since it was her dancing that had caused their group to fall apart eight years ago.

Besides, they only saw what she wanted them to see. If you took her social media pages and her website at face value then she was living the creative dream. What they *didn't* know was that Chantal cut out all the dark, unseemly bits she wasn't proud of: her nasty divorce, her empty bank account, the reasons why she'd booked into some small-time gig on the coast when she should be concentrating on getting back into a proper dance company...

'Thanks, Willa. How's that brother of yours? Is he still overseas?' She hoped the change of topic wasn't too no-ticeable.

'Luke texted me today. He's working on some big deal, but it looks like he might be coming home soon.' Willa sighed. 'We might be able to get the whole gang back together after all.'

The 'whole gang' was the tight-knit crew that had formed when they'd all worked together at the magical Weeping Reef resort in the Whitsundays. Had it really been eight years ago? She still remembered it as vividly as if it were yesterday. The ocean had been so blue it had seemed otherworldly, the sand had been almost pure white, and she'd loved every second of it... Right until she'd screwed it all up.

'Maybe,' Chantal said.

'I think we might even be getting some of the group together tonight.' There was a meaningful pause on the other end of the line. 'If you're free, we'd love to see you.'

'Sorry, Willa, I'm actually working tonight.'

Chantal checked the road signs and took the on-ramp leading out of the city. Sydney sparkled in her rearview mirror as she sped away.

'Oh? Anywhere close by?'

'I'm afraid not. I'm off to Newcastle for this one.'

'Oh, right. Any place I would know?'

'Not likely, it's called Nine East. It's a small theatre—very intimate.'

She forced herself to sound excited when really she wanted to find a secluded island and hide until her dancing ability came back. God only knew why she'd given Willa the place's name. She prayed her friend wouldn't look it up online.

'Look, Willa, I'll have to cut you short. I'm on the road and I need my full concentration to deal with these crazy Sydney drivers.'

Willa chuckled. 'I forget sometimes that you didn't grow up in the city. Hopefully we'll catch up soon?'

The hope in her voice caused a twinge of guilt in Chantal's stomach. She didn't want to see the group. Rather, she didn't want them to see how her life was not what she'd made it out to be.

'Yeah, hopefully.'

There was nothing like being surrounded by friends, with the sea air running over your skin and a cold drink in your hand. Add to that the city lights bouncing off the water's surface and a view of the Sydney Harbour Bridge against an inky night and you had a damn near perfect evening.

Brodie Mitchell leant back against the railing of his yacht and surveyed the group in front of him. Champagne flowed, music wafted up into the air and the group was laughing and reminiscing animatedly about their time working at the Weeping Reef resort. A long time had passed, but it made Brodie smile to think the group was no less lively now than when they'd all been fresh-faced kids, drunk on the freedom and beauty of resort life.

'Hey, man.' Scott Knight dropped down beside him, beer in hand. 'Aren't you drinking tonight?'

'I'm trying to be good for once.' Brodie grinned and held up his bottle of water in salute. 'I'm training for a half marathon.'

'Really?' Scott raised a brow.

Brodie shoved his friend and laughed. 'Yes, really.'

As much as he wanted to be annoyed that his friends would assume him incapable of running a half marathon, he kind of saw their point. Running competitively required a certain kind of routine and dedication that wasn't Brodie's style. He was a laid-back kind of guy: he thrived on surf, sand, and girls in bikinis. Abstaining from alcohol and waking up at the crack of dawn for training... Not so much.

'You have to admit it doesn't seem to fit in with the yachting lifestyle.' Scott gestured to the scenery around them.

The boat was a sight to behold—luxury in every sense of the word from its classy interior design to the quality craftsmanship out on the deck.

Growing up in a big family had meant the Mitchells' weekly grocery shop had needed to stretch across many mouths, and schoolbooks had always been passed down the line. They hadn't been poor, but he'd never been exposed to fineries such as yachts. Now he owned a yacht charter business and had several boats to his name.

'I didn't exactly come up with the idea myself,' Brodie admitted, taking a swig of his water. 'There's a guy at the marina back home and he's always on my back about taking up running. He bet me a hundred bucks I couldn't train for a race.'

'So you started with a half marathon?' Scott shook his head, laughing. 'Why not attempt a lazy ten k to begin with?'

Brodie shrugged and grinned at his friend. 'If I'm going to waste a perfectly good sleep-in, it might as well be for something big.'

'Says the guy who once chose sleep over judging a bikini contest.'

'And lived to regret it.'

Scott interlocked his fingers behind his head and leant back against the boat's railings. 'Those were the days.'

'You look like you're living the dream now.' Brodie fought to keep a note of envy out of his voice.

A slow grin spread over Scott's face as his fiancée, Kate, waved from the makeshift dance floor where she was shaking her hips with Willa, Amy, and Amy's friend Jessica. The girls were laughing and dancing, champagne in hand. *Just like old times.*

'I am.' Scott nodded solemnly.

Just as Brodie was about to change the topic of conversation Willa broke away from the group and joined the boys. She dropped down next to Brodie and slung her arm around his shoulders, giving him a sisterly squeeze as she pushed her dark hair out of her face.

'I'm so glad you're back down in Sydney,' Willa said.

'And where's your man tonight?' Brodie asked.

'Working.' She pouted. 'But he promised he'd be here next time. In fact I think he was a little pissed to miss out on the yacht experience.'

Brodie chuckled. 'It's an experience, indeed. My clients pay an arm and a leg to be sailed around in this boat, and she's an absolute beauty. Worth every cent.'

The *Princess 56* certainly fitted her name, and although she was the oldest of the yachts his company owned she'd aged as gracefully as a silver-screen starlet. He patted the railing affectionately.

'Guess who I spoke to this afternoon,' Willa said, cutting into his thoughts with a faux innocent smile.

Brodie quirked a brow. 'Who?'

'Chantal.'

Hearing her name was enough to set Brodie's blood pumping harder. Chantal Turner was the only girl ever to have held his attention for longer than five minutes. She'd been the life of the party during their time at the Whitsundays, and she'd had a magnetic force that had drawn people to her like flies to honey. And, boy, had he been sucked in! The only problem was, she'd been Scott's girl back then. He'd gotten too close to her, played with fire, and earned a black eye for it. Worse still, he'd lost his friend for the better part of eight years over the incident.

Brodie's eyes flicked to Scott, but there was no tension in his face. He was too busy perving on Kate to be worrying about what Willa said.

'She's got a show on tonight,' Willa continued. 'Just up the coast.'

Brodie swallowed. The last thing he needed was to see Chantal Turner dance. The way she moved was enough to bring grown men to their knees, and he had a particular weakness for girls who knew how to move.

'We could head there—since we have the boat.' Willa grinned and nudged him with her elbow.

'How do you know where she's performing?' he asked, taking another swig of his water to alleviate the dryness in his mouth.

'She told me.'

'I don't know if we should…' Brodie forced a slow breath, trying to shut down images of his almost-kiss with Chantal.

It was the last time he'd seen her—though there had been a few nights when he'd been home alone and he'd looked her performances up online. He wasn't sure what seeing her in person would do to his resolve to leave the past in the past.

The friend zone was something to be respected, and girls who landed themselves in that zone never came out. But with Chantal he seemed to lose control over his ability to think straight.

'We should go,' Scott said, patting Brodie on the shoulder as if to reassure him once again that there were no hard feelings about that night. 'I'm sure she'd appreciate the crowd support.'

By this time Amy, Jessica, and Kate had wandered over for a refill. Scott, ever the gentleman, grabbed the bottle of vintage brut and topped everyone up.

'We were just talking about taking a little trip up the coast,' Scott said. 'Chantal has a show on.'

'Oh, we should definitely go!' Amy said, and the other girls nodded their agreement.

All eyes lay expectantly on him. He could manage a simple reunion. Couldn't he…?

'Why the hell not?' he said, pushing up from his chair.

* * *

When Chantal pulled into the car park of the location specified on her email confirmation her heart sank. The job had been booked last-minute—*they'd* contacted *her*, with praise for the performance snippets she had on her website and an offer of work for a few nights a week over the next month.

A cursory look at their website hadn't given her much: it seemed they did a mix of dance and music, including an open mike night once per week. Not exactly ideal, but she was desperate. So she'd accepted the offer and put her focus back on her auditions, thinking nothing of it.

Except it didn't look like the quietly elegant bar on their website. The sign was neon red, for starters, and there were several rough-looking men hanging out at the front, smoking. Chantal bit down on her lip. Everything in her gut told her to turn around and head home—but how could she do that when it was the only gig she'd been able to book in weeks? Make that months.

Sighing, she straightened her shoulders. *Don't be such a snob. You know the arts industry includes all types. They're probably not criminals at all.*

But the feeling of dismay grew stronger with each step she took towards the entrance. She hitched her bag higher on her shoulder and fought back the wave of negativity. She *had* to take this job. Her ex had finally sold the apartment—meaning she had to find a new place to live—and this job included on-site accommodation. It would leave her days free to pursue more auditions, *and* it was money that she desperately needed right now.

One of the men hanging out at the front of the bar leered at her as she hurried past, and Chantal wished she'd thrown on a pair of tracksuit pants over her dancing shorts. The sun was setting in the distance but the air was still heavy and warm. She ignored the wolf-whistling and continued on, head held high, into the bar.

The stench of cheap alcohol hit her first, forcing her stomach to dip and dive. A stage sat in the middle of a room and three men in all-black outfits fiddled with the sound equipment. Chantal looked around, surveying the sorry sight that was to be her home for the next month. The soles of her sneakers sucked with each step along the tattered, faded carpet—as if years of grime had left behind an adhesive layer. Though smoking had long been banned inside bars, a faint whiff of stale cigarette smoke still hung in the air. A small boot-sized hole had broken the plaster of one wall and a cracked light flickered overhead.

Delightful.

She approached the bar, mustering a smile as she tried to catch the attention of the older man drying wineglasses and hanging them in a rack above his head. 'Excuse me, I'm here—'

'Dancers go upstairs,' he said, without even looking up from his work.

'Thanks,' she muttered, turning on her heel and making her way towards the stairs at the end of the bar.

Upstairs can't possibly be any worse than downstairs. Perhaps the downstairs was for bands only? Maybe the dancers' section would be a little more…hygienic?

Chantal trod up the last few steps, trying her utmost to be positive. But upstairs *wasn't* any better.

'Oh, crap.'

The stage in the middle of the room sported a large silver pole. The stage itself was round with seats encircling it; a faded red curtain hung at the back, parted only where the dancers would enter and exit from. It was a bloody strip club!

'Chantal?'

A voice caught her attention. She contemplated lying

for a second, but the recognition on the guy's face told her he knew *exactly* who she was.

'Hi.'

'I've got your room key, but I don't have time to show you where it is now.' He looked her up and down, the heavy lines at the corners of his eyes crinkling slightly. 'Just head out back and get ready with the other girls.'

'Uh…I think there's been some kind of mistake. I'm not a stripper.'

'Sure you're not, darlin',' he said with a raspy chuckle. 'I get it—you're an *artist*. Most of the girls say they're paying their way through university, but whatever floats your boat.'

'I'm serious. I don't take my clothes off.' She shook her head, fighting the rising pressure in her chest.

'And we're not technically a strip club. Think of it more as…burlesque.' He thrust the room key into her hand. 'You'll fit right in.'

Chantal bit down on her lip. Perhaps it wouldn't be as bad as she thought.

But, no matter how hard she tried to convince herself, her gut pleaded with her to leave.

'I really don't think this is going to work,' she said, holding the key out to him.

'You *really* should have thought of that before sending back our contract with your signature on it.' His eyes hardened, thin lips pressing into a harsh line. 'But I can have our lawyer settle this, if you still think this isn't going to work.'

The thinly veiled threat made Chantal's heartbeat kick up a notch. There was no way she could afford a lawyer if they decided to take her to court. How could she have made such a colossal mistake?

Her head pounded, signalling a migraine that would no doubt materialise at some point. What kind of club had a lawyer on call, anyway? *The dangerous kind...the kind that has enough work for a lawyer.*

'Fine.' She dropped her hand by her side and forced away the desire to slap the club owner across his smarmy, wrinkled face.

She was a big girl—she could handle this. Besides, she'd had her fair share of promo girl gigs whilst trying out for dance schools the first time. She'd strutted around in tiny shorts to sell energy drinks and race-car merchandise on more than one occasion. This wouldn't be so different...would it?

Sighing, she made her way to the change room where the other dancers were getting ready. She still had that funny, niggling feeling that something wasn't quite right... and it wasn't *just* that she'd somehow landed herself in a strip club.

She concentrated for a moment, analysing the feeling. It had grown stronger since her audition—an incessant tugging of her senses that wouldn't abate. She unpacked her make-up and plucked a face wipe from her bag. Smoothing the cloth over her face, she thought back to the director. He'd looked so familiar, and he hadn't seemed to be able to look her in the eye.

A memory crashed into her with such force she stopped in her tracks, hand in midair. An old photo, taken a few years before she'd first started dating Derek—*that* was where she'd seen his face before. He was a friend of her ex-husband's, and that *couldn't* be a coincidence.

Rage surged through her. Her hands trembling, she sorted through her make-up for foundation. That smarmy, good-for-nothing ex-husband of hers had put her name forward for this skanky bar. He probably found the idea hilarious.

If I ever come across that spiteful SOB again I'm going to kill him!

* * *

An hour and a half later Chantal prepared to go on stage. She looked at herself in the mirror, hoping to hell that it was the fluorescent lighting which made her look white as a ghost and just as sickly. But the alarming contrast against her dark eye make-up and glossed lips would look great under the stage lighting. She'd seem alluring, mysterious.

Not that any of the patrons of such a bar would be interested in 'mysterious'. No, she assumed it was a 'more is more' kind of place.

She sighed, smoothing her hair out of her face and adding a touch of hairspray to the front so it didn't fall into her eyes. The other dancers seemed friendly, and there *were* actually two burlesque performers—though they didn't look as if they danced on the mainstream circuit. When she'd asked if all the dancers stripped down she'd received a wink and an unexpected view of the older lady's 'pasties'.

Well, *she* wouldn't be taking off her clothes—though her outfit wasn't exactly covering much of her body anyway. She looked down at the top which wrapped around her bust and rib cage in thick black strips, and at the matching shorts that barely came down to her thighs. She might as well have been naked for how exposed she felt.

It wasn't normal for her to be so filled with nerves before going onstage. But butterflies warmed her stomach and her every breath was more ragged than the last. She pressed her fingertips to her temples and shut her eyes, concentrating on relaxing her breathing. After a few attempts hcr heart rate slowed, and the air was coming more easily into her lungs.

Her act would be different—and she wouldn't be dancing for the audience…she would be dancing for herself. Taking a deep breath, she hovered at the entrance to the stage, waiting for the dancer before her to finish.

It was now or never.

CHAPTER TWO

'ARE YOU SURE we're in the right place?' Brodie looked around the run-down bar and shook his head. 'She can't be dancing *here*.'

'I double-checked the address,' Willa said, her dark brows pinched into a frown. 'This is definitely it.'

'Looks like there's an upstairs section to this place.' Kate pointed to a set of stairs on the other side of the room.

A single guy sat in the middle of the stage, playing old country-and-western hits, his voice not quite up to par. The bottom half of the bar was crowded and Brodie stayed close to the girls, given a few of the patrons were looking at them a little too closely for his liking. The group wove through the crowd until they reached the staircase at the back of the room, filing one by one up to the next level.

The music changed from the twangy country-and-western songs to a more sensual bass-heavy grind. The crowd—all men—encircled the stage and were enthusiastically cheering on a blonde dancer performing on a pole. She wore little more than a glittering turquoise bikini and her feet were balanced precariously on the highest pair of heels Brodie had ever seen.

'We *must* be in the wrong place.' Brodie rubbed his fingers to his temple, forcing down the worry bubbling in his chest.

Willa shrugged, looking as confused as he felt.

Chantal was a magnificent dancer—he'd often sneaked away from his duties at the Weeping Reef resort when he'd known she'd be using her time off to practise. She had innate skill and passion when she danced, no matter if it was in a studio or on the resort's packed dance floor. He couldn't understand why on earth she would be wasting her talent performing at some dingy dive bar.

The blonde left the stage to a roar of approval from the crowd and the music faded from one song to the next. His eyes were riveted to the space between the red curtains at the back of the stage. Heart in his throat, he willed the next dancer to be anyone else in the world other than Chantal. But the second a figure emerged from the darkness he knew it was her. He felt her before his eyes confirmed it.

No one else had a pair of legs like hers—so long and lean and mouth-wateringly flexible. She took her time coming to the front of the stage, her hips swinging in time to the music. Each step forward revealed a little more as she approached the spotlight. Long dark hair tumbled in messy waves around her shoulders, swishing as she moved. The ends were lightened from too much sun and her limbs were bronzed, without a tan line in sight.

Her eyes seemed to focus on nothing, and the dark make-up made her look like every dirty, sexy, disturbing fantasy he'd ever had. A jolt of arousal shot through him, burning and making his skin prickle with awareness.

He was in a dream—that *had* to be it. It was the only plausible explanation for how he'd ended up in this hellish alternative universe where he was forced to watch his deepest fantasy come to life right in front of him. He'd never been able to keep his mind off Chantal at the resort, but now she was here, the ultimate temptation, and he had to watch a hundred other men ogle her as though she were a piece of meat offered up for their dining pleasure.

His fists balled by his sides as he fought the urge to

rush up onto the stage and carry her away. She wasn't his responsibility, and the more distance he kept the better. He'd learnt that lesson already.

A wolf-whistle erupted from the crowd, snatching Brodie's attention away from his inner turmoil. Chantal had one hand on the pole, and though she wasn't using it as a prop, the way her fingers slid up and down the silver length made the front of his pants tighten. He shut his eyes for a moment, willing the excitement to stop. He shouldn't be feeling as if he wanted to steal her away and devour her whole...but he did.

When he dared to open his eyes he found himself looking straight into the endless depths of Chantal's luminous olive-green gaze. Emotion flickered across her face and her mouth snapped shut as she continued to dance, her eyes locked straight onto him.

Was it his imagination or were her cheeks a little pinker than before? For a moment he let himself believe she danced only for him, each gentle curve of movement designed to bring him undone.

In that moment she was *his*.

Dancing barefoot, she moved about the stage as though she owned it. Her feet pointed and flexed, creating lines and artful movement. Her arms floated above her head, crossing at the wrists before opening out into a graceful arc. Brodie's body hummed as though she played him with each step, with each look, each flick of her hair.

Her eyes remained on him. She seduced him. Broke apart every brick of resolve that he'd put in place until the wall crumbled around him like a house crushed by a tidal wave.

She capsized him. Bewitched him.

Her eyes glimmered under the spotlight, energy building with the climax of her performance. His body tensed and excitement wound tight within him. A coil of wanting, ready to be released at any moment. It was so wrong. He'd thought he'd moved on. Forgotten her. What a joke. He'd never get Chantal out of his head. *Never.*

The spell was broken as soon as her song finished. Her eyes locked on him for one final moment before she retreated behind the red curtain. The catcalls and cheering only made Brodie's pulse increase and tension tighten in his limbs. She should *not* be dancing in a place like this. Wasn't she supposed to be married? Where the hell was her husband and why wasn't he protecting her?

'That wasn't quite what I expected,' Willa said, looking from Amy to Brodie and back again. 'I mean, she's a gorgeous dancer—but this place is…'

'Wrong.' Brodie gritted his teeth together.

'Don't be so judgmental, you two.' Amy folded her arms across her chest. 'I'm going to see if I can find out what time she finishes.'

She wandered off in the direction of the stage but Brodie hung back with the others. Scott and Kate were chatting and laughing amongst themselves; Willa and Jessica were discussing the outfit of the next performer. Brodie leant back against the wall and ran a hand through his hair. His heart thudded an erratic beat and he wasn't sure if it was from the desire to protect Chantal or from the fact that her skimpy black outfit had worked his libido into overdrive.

No, it had to be concern over her safety. He had four little sisters, and the need to protect was ingrained in him as deep as his need to breathe. Sure he was attracted to Chantal—what red-blooded man wouldn't be? But it was nothing more than that. It had *never* been more than that.

Somehow the lie was no more believable now than it had been eight years ago.

Chantal had thought it wasn't possible for the night to get any worse. Dancing in front of a room full of people who wouldn't know art if it hit them over the head was bad enough, and the catcalls and leering were the proverbial cherry. But then she'd spotted Brodie and a good chunk of the Weeping Reef gang. Her stomach had felt as if it had dropped straight through the stage floor.

She braced her hands at the edge of the make-up bench and looked at herself in the mirror. All she wanted was to wash off her make-up and lock herself away until humiliation lost its brutal edge…though it was possible that would take a while. The shock on his face had been enough to destroy whatever confidence she'd managed to build up. He'd looked at her with an unnerving combination of disbelief and hunger.

She was about to remove her false lashes when her name rang out amongst the backstage hustle and bustle. Amy bounded towards her, arms outstretched and shiny blond hair flying around her face.

'You were fantastic!' Amy threw her arms around Chantal and gave her a friendly squeeze.

'Thanks.' Chantal forced a smile, wishing for possibly the hundredth time since she'd met Amy that she could have even an ounce of her vivacious confidence. 'It's a small gig in between a few bigger things.'

She hoped the lie didn't sound as hollow out in the open as it did in her head, but she couldn't let go of the false image she'd constructed. If they knew how bad things were right now… She wouldn't be able to handle the pity. Pity was the thing she detested most in life—possibly due to the fact that it had been doled out in epic proportions throughout her childhood.

The teachers had pitied her and her borrowed schoolbooks, the other mums and their suit-and-tie husbands had pitied the way she'd had to wear the same clothes week after week, and as for the students…pity from her peers had always stung the most.

'No judgment here.' Amy held up her hands. 'You have to come for a drink with us, though. We've got everyone together…well, almost everyone.'

'Oh, I would love to, but…' Chantal's smile wavered. 'It's been a long day and I've got an audition tomorrow.'

She scrambled for an excuse—something that Amy wouldn't question. There was no way she could go out there and face them—no way she could keep her head held high after what they'd seen. Heat crawled up her neck, squeezing the air from her throat. *Not now, please don't fall apart now.*

'Is your audition in Newcastle?'

'No, Sydney. So I've got quite a long drive.'

Amy grinned and grabbed her hand, tugging her towards the door. 'I've got the perfect solution then. Brodie got us here on his yacht, but he's supposed to be docking at The Rocks. If your rehearsal is in the city it would be perfect. You won't have to drive there, and Brodie can sail you back here after your audition.'

'I really *am* tired.' She shook her head and pulled her hand from Amy's grasp.

'You just need a drink or five.' Amy winked. 'Come on—it'll be like old times.'

Chantal stole a glance at her reflection. She'd have to change. There was no way she'd go out there and stand in front of Brodie wearing mere scraps of Lycra. *It's not like he didn't notice you dancing half-naked on that stage.*

'Just one drink,' she said, sighing. 'I need to be on good form tomorrow.'

'Great.' Amy bounced on the spot. 'I'll let you get changed. Meet us out the front in a few minutes?'

'Sure.'

With Amy gone, Chantal could let the fake smile slide from her lips. Why the hell had she agreed to a drink with the old gang? She was supposed to be keeping her distance—at least until her life had started to match the image she'd presented online. No doubt they'd ask about her marriage: fail number one. They'd want to know about her career: fail number two. And she'd have to act as if it wasn't awkward at *all* being around Scott and Brodie: fail number three.

Willa had told her that they'd recently repaired the rift she'd caused, but that didn't make her any less squeamish about having the two of them in the same room as her.

She contemplated looking for a back exit to slip out of. Maybe if she disappeared they might get the hint that she wasn't feeling social right now.

You can't do that. These people are your friends...possibly your only friends.

Since her divorce her other acquaintances had been mysteriously absent. Perhaps being friends with Derek the talent agent was of more value to them than being friends with Chantal the out-of-work dancer.

She frowned at herself in the mirror, taking in the fake lashes and dark, sultry make-up. What a fraud. Sighing, she stripped out of her outfit and threw on her denim shorts, white tank top and sneakers from earlier. She didn't have time to remove all of her make-up—that tedious task would have to wait for later.

Swinging her overnight bag over one shoulder, she decided against dumping it in her room first. If she found the comfort of a private room it would be unlikely she'd come back out. *Suck it up, Chantal. You've made your bed, now lie in it!*

Outside the crowd heaved, and she had to dodge the patrons who thought their ticket to the show meant they had a right to paw at her. This was *not* the dream she'd had in mind when she'd first stepped into a dance studio at the age of seven.

Her skin crawled. She wanted out of this damn filthy

bar. Perhaps a potential lawsuit was worth the risk if it meant she never had to come back.

She was midthought when she spotted Brodie, standing alone by the stairs. Where had everyone else gone? Her blood pumped harder, fuelling her limbs with nervous energy.

As always, his presence unnerved her. His broad shoulders and muscular arms were barely contained in a fitted white T-shirt; his tanned skin beckoned to be touched. His shaggy blond hair sat slightly shorter than it had used to, though the ends were still sun-bleached and he wore it as though he'd spent the day windsurfing. Messy. Touchable.

But it was his eyes that always got her. Crystal green, like the colour of polished jade, they managed to seem scorching hot and ice-cold at the same time. When he looked at her it was easy to pretend the rest of the world didn't exist.

'The others have gone to the boat,' he said, motioning for her to join him. 'I didn't want you to walk on your own.'

She followed him, watching the way his butt moved beneath a pair of well-worn jeans. He'd filled out since she'd seen him last—traded his boy's body for one which was undeniably adult. She licked her lips, hating the attraction that flared in her and threatened to burn wild, like a fire out of control.

It was strange to be attracted to someone again. She hadn't felt that way in a long time...possibly not since Weeping Reef. Her marriage hadn't been about attraction—it had been about safety, security... Until that security had started to feel like walls crushing in on her.

They made their way out of the bar and into the cool night air. The breeze caught her sweat-dampened skin and caused goosebumps to ripple across her arms. She folded them tight, feeling vulnerable and exposed in the sudden quiet of the outdoors.

'You didn't have to wait,' she said, falling into step with him.

Their steps echoed in the quiet night air, their strides perfectly matched.

He turned to her and shook his head. 'Of course I did. I was worried you wouldn't make it out of the bar on your own, let alone down the street.'

The disapproving tone in his voice made her stomach twist. The last thing she needed was another overprotective man in her life.

'I can take care of myself.'

'Your bravado is admirable, but pointless. Even the smallest guy in there would have at least a head on you.'

His face softened into a smile—he never had been the kind of guy who could stay in a bad mood for long.

'Not to mention those skinny little chicken legs of yours.'

'I do *not* have chicken legs.' She gave him a shove and he barely broke stride, instead throwing his head back and laughing.

The bubble of anxiety in her chest dissolved. Brodie *always* had that effect on her. He was an irritating, lazy charmer, who talked his way through life, but he was *fun*. She often found herself smiling at him even when she wanted to be annoyed—much to her chagrin.

'No, you don't have chicken legs…not any more.' He grinned, his perfect teeth flashing in the night. 'You grew up.'

'So did you,' she said, but the words were lost as a motorcycle raced down the road.

They had eight years and a lot of issues between them. *Issues*, of course, was a code word for attraction. But *issues* sounded a little more benign and a little less like a prelude to something she would regret.

'I thought your husband would be here to watch out

for you.' He was back to being stern again. 'He should be keeping you safe.'

'I think he's keeping someone else safe these days.' She sighed. Why did all guys think it was their job to be the protector? She'd been happy to see the back of her ex-husband and his stifling, control-freak ways.

'So that means you're single?'

She nodded. 'Free as a bird and loving it.'

'All the more reason to have someone look out for you.'

Chantal bit her down on her lip and kept her mouth shut. No sense in firing him up by debating her ability to look out for herself. She wasn't stupid, her mother had made her take self-defence classes in high school, and she was quite sure she could hit a guy where it hurt most should the need arise.

They walked in silence for a moment, the thumping bass from the bar fading as they moved farther away. The yacht club glowed up ahead, with one large boat sticking out amongst a row of much smaller ones. She didn't have to ask. Of *course* he had the biggest boat there.

'Are you over-compensating?' Chantal asked, using sarcasm to hide her nervousness at being so close to him…at being alone with him.

'Huh?'

'The boat.' She pointed. 'It's rather…large.'

'You know what they say about men with large boats.' He grinned, his perfect teeth gleaming against the inky darkness.

She stifled a wicked smile. 'They have large steering wheels?'

He threw his head back and laughed again, slinging an arm around her shoulder.

The sudden closeness of him unsettled her, but his presence was wonderfully intoxicating when he wasn't waxing lyrical about her need for protection. He smelled exactly the same as she remembered: ocean spray and coconut. That scent had haunted her for months after she'd left Weeping Reef, and any time she smelled a hint of coconut it would thrust her right back onto that dance floor with him.

Her hip bumped against his with each step. The hard muscles of his arm pressed around her shoulder, making her insides curl and jump.

'It's not my personal boat. My company owns it.'

'Your company?' Chantal looked up, surprised.

Brodie was not the kind of guy to start a company; he'd never had an entrepreneurial bone in his body. In fact she distinctly remembered the time Scott had threatened to fire him for going over time on his windsurfing lessons because his students had been having so much fun. He had a generosity of spirit that didn't exactly match bottom-line profits.

'After I left Weeping Reef I bummed around for a while until I got work with a yacht charter company off the Sunshine Coast. It was a lot of fun. I got promoted, and eventually the owners offered me a stake in the company. I bought the controlling share about a year ago, when they were ready to retire.'

'And now you run a yacht tour company?'

He nodded as their conversation was interrupted by a loud shriek as they strolled onto the marina. The girls had clearly got into the champagne and were dancing on deck, with an amused Scott watching from the sidelines. Willa waved down to her and motioned for them to join the party.

Chantal's old doubts and fears crept back, their dark claws hooking into the parts of her not yet healed. She was not the person she claimed to be, and they would all know that now. They would know what a *fraud* she was.

Her breath caught in her throat, the familiar shallow breathing returning and forcing her heart rate up. She had a sudden desire to flee, to return to the dingy bar where she probably looked as if she belonged.

She didn't fit in here. Not with these classy girls and their beautiful hair. Not with Brodie, who'd made a success of himself, and not with Scott, whom she'd betrayed.

She sucked in a deep breath, her feet rooted to the ground. Panic clutched at her chest, clawing up her neck and closing its cold hands around her windpipe. She couldn't do it.

'Chantal?' Brodie looked down at her, his hand at the small of her back, pushing gently.

She bit down on her lip, shame seeping through her every limb until they were so heavy she couldn't move. *Why did you come? You're only setting yourself up to be laughed at. You're a failure.*

'Come on.' Brodie grabbed her hand and tugged her forward. 'We don't want to get left behind.'

CHAPTER THREE

BRODIE WANTED TO look anywhere but at Chantal, yet her dancing held him captive. Her undulating figure, moving perfectly to the beat, looked even more amazing than it had at the bar. In casual clothes, with her face relaxed, her limbs loose, she looked completely at ease with the world.

Unable to deal with the lust flooding his veins, he'd caved in and had a beer. The alcohol had hit him a little harder since he'd been abstaining the past few weeks. But he needed to dull the edges of his feelings—dull the roaring awareness of her. He'd hoped the uncontrollable desire to possess her had disappeared when he'd left the reef. However, it had only been dormant, waiting quietly in the background, until she'd brought it to full-colour, surround-sound, 3-D life.

When they'd first stepped onto the yacht Chantal had hesitated, almost as if she wasn't sure she should be there. But Scott had given her a friendly pat on the shoulder and a playful shove towards the girls. They'd brought her into the fold and she'd relaxed, dancing and giggling as though she'd been there all night. Every so often Brodie caught her eye: a quick glance here or there that neither of them acknowledged.

'You should get out there and dance with her.' Scott dropped down next to him, another beer in his hand.

Brodie's eyes shifted to Scott and he waited to see what

would come next. He'd harboured a lot of guilt over the way things had ended between them at Weeping Reef—not just because he'd hurt Scott, but because he'd hurt Chantal as well.

'Come on, man. You know there's no hard feelings.' Scott slapped him on the back. 'We talked about this already.'

'It's not your feelings I'm worried about.'

'Since when do you worry about anything?'

Brodie frowned. People often took his breezy attitude and laissez-faire approach to mean he didn't care about things. He knew when Scott was teasing him, but still...

'Some things are meant to be left in the past.' Some *people* were meant to be left in the past...especially when he couldn't possibly give her what she deserved. Not long-term anyway.

'You sound like a girl.' Scott laughed. 'Don't be such a wuss.'

He *was* being a wuss, hiding behind excuses. Besides, it was only a dance. How much harm could it do?

Keep telling yourself it's harmless—maybe one day you'll believe it.

Brodie pushed aside his gut feeling and joined the girls. Loud music pumped from the yacht's premium speakers and the girls cheered when he joined their little circle. His eyes caught Chantal's—a flicker of inquisitive olive as she looked him over and then turned her head so that she faced Amy.

He took a long swig of his beer, draining the bottle and setting it out of the way. Moving closer to Chantal, he brushed his hand gently over her hip as he danced. She turned, a shy smile curving on her lips. She wasn't performing now—this was her and only her. Green eyes seemed to glow amidst the smudgy black make-up... Her tanned limbs were moving subtly and effortlessly to the beat.

'Want a refill?' Brodie nodded to the empty champagne flute she'd yet to discard.

She hesitated, looking from the glass to him. Was it his imagination, or had Willa given her a little nudge with her elbow?

'Why not?' She smiled and followed him into the cabin. The music seemed to throb and pulsate around them, even at a distance from the speakers. But that was how music felt when she moved to it. It came to life.

'I'm sad to say this yacht is bigger than my apartment.' She held out her champagne flute. 'Well, my old apartment anyway.'

Brodie reached for a fresh bottle of Veuve Cliquot and wrapped his hand around the cork, easing it out with a satisfying pop. He topped up her glass, the fizzing liquid bubbling and racing towards the top a little too quickly.

She bent her head and caught the bubbles before they spilled. 'You're a terrible pourer.'

He watched, mesmerised, as the pink tip of her tongue darted out to swipe her lips. Her mouth glistened, tempting and ripe as summer fruit.

'I'm normally too busy driving the boat to be in charge of drinks. But I'll make an exception for you.'

'How kind.' She smirked and leant against the white leather sofa that curved around the wall. 'Are you always on the boats?'

'No, I have to run the business, which keeps me from being out on the water as much as I'd like. I have a town-house on the Sunshine Coast, but it's a bit of a tourist trap up there. Sometimes I stay with the family in Brisbane, and then other times I stay on the yacht.'

'What a life.' Her voice was soft, tinged with wonder. 'You float along and stop where you feel like it.'

'It has a little more structure than that...but essentially, yeah.'

'Now, *that* sounds a little more like the Brodie I know.'

Her words needled him. He *wasn't* the surfer bum loser she'd labelled him in Weeping Reef. Sure, he might have dropped out of his degree and taken his time to find his groove, but he was a business owner now…a successful one at that.

'How's the arts world treating you?' It could have sounded like a swipe, given what he'd seen tonight, but he was genuinely interested.

She managed a stiff smile. 'Like any creative industry, it can be a little up and down.'

A perfectly generic response. Perhaps her situation was worse than he'd thought. He stayed silent, waiting for her to continue. For a moment she only nodded, her head bobbing, as if that would be enough of an answer. But he wanted more.

'I'm waiting to hear back from a big company,' she continued, her voice tight.

He suspected it wasn't true, or that she'd coloured the truth.

'Tonight was one of those fill-the-gap things. I'm sure it wasn't what you were expecting to see.'

Her eyes dipped and her lashes, thick and sultry, fanned out, casting feathery shadows against her cheekbones. She gathered herself and looked up, determined once more.

'It *wasn't* what I expected,' Brodie said, watching her face for subtle movements. Any key to whether or not she would let him in. 'But that's not to say I didn't enjoy it.'

How could he possibly have felt any other way? Watching her work that stage as if she owned the place had unsettled him to his core. A thousand years wouldn't dull that picture from his memory. Even thinking about it now heated up his skin and sent a rush of blood south, hardening him instantaneously.

'I could have done without the men ogling you.'

Her lips curved ever so slightly. 'You say that like you have some kind of claim over me.'

It was a taunt, delivered in her soft way. She hit him hardest when she used that breathy little voice of hers. It sounded like sin and punishment and all kinds of heavenly temptation rolled into one.

Brodie stepped forward, indulging himself in the sight of her widening eyes and parted lips. She didn't step back. Instead she stilled, and the air between them was charged with untameable electricity—wild and crackling and furious as a stormy ocean. She tilted her head up, looking him directly in the eye.

Brodie leant forward. 'I did see you first.'

'It doesn't work like that.' Her voice was a mere whisper, and she said it as though convincing herself. 'It's not finders keepers.'

'What is it, then?'

'It's *nothing*.'

He grabbed her wrist, his fingers wrapping around the delicate joint so that his fingertips lay over the tender flesh on the inside of her arm. He could feel her pulse hammering like a pump working at full speed, the beats furious and insistent.

'It's not nothing.'

She tried to pull her wrist back. 'It's the champagne.'

'Liar.'

A wicked smile broke out across her face as she downed her entire drink. A stray droplet escaped the corner of her mouth and she caught it with her tongue. God, he wanted to kiss her.

'It's the *champagne*.'

'Well, if you keep drinking it like that...'

'I might get myself into trouble?' She pulled a serious face, her cheeks flushed with the alcohol.

She'd looked like this the night he'd danced with her at

Weeping Reef. Chantal had always been the serious type—studious and sensible until she'd had a drink or two. Then the hardness seemed to melt away, she loosened up, and the playful side came out. If she'd been tempting before, she was damn near impossible to resist now.

'You always seem to treat trouble like it's a bad idea.' He divested her of her champagne flute before tugging her to him.

'Isn't that the definition of trouble?' Her hands hovered at his chest, barely touching him.

He shouldn't be pulling her strings the way he usually did when he wanted a girl. He liked to wind them up first. Tease them...get them to laugh. Relax their boundaries. He was treating Chantal as if he wanted to sleep with her...and he did.

He was in for a world of pain, but he couldn't stop himself.

'Bad ideas are the most fun.'

She stepped backwards, cheeks flushed, lips pursed. 'Come on—we're missing all the action out there. I want to dance.'

Only someone like Brodie would think bad ideas were fun. She could list her bad ideas like a how-to guide for stuffing up your life—have the hots for your boyfriend's BFF, pick the wrong guy to marry, lose focus on your career.

No, bad ideas were most definitely *not* fun.

Brodie was smoking hot, and it was clear that their chemistry still sizzled like nothing else, but that didn't mean she could indulge herself. He was *still* a bad idea, and she'd established that bad ideas were a thing of the past... well, once she'd got out of her current contract anyway.

If only she could tell her heart to stop thudding as if a dubstep track ran through her body, then she would be on her way to being fine. The throbbing between her legs was another matter entirely.

She stepped onto the deck, wondering for a moment if she'd dreamed herself onto his boat. The ocean had been engulfed by the night, but the air still held a salty tang. The smell reminded her of home…and of Brodie.

Shaking her head, she approached the girls. Kate extended her hand to Chantal and drew her in. She had decided almost immediately that she liked the gorgeous, witty redhead, and it was clear neither she nor Scott held any ill feelings towards her. It was a relief, all things considered.

'And where were *you*?' Willa eyed her with a salacious grin, her cheeks pink from champagne and dancing. She brushed her heavy fringe out of her eyes and swayed to the music.

'Just getting a refill.' The champagne was still fresh on her tongue…her mind was blurred pleasantly around the edges.

'Riiiight.' Willa smirked.

Chantal could feel Brodie close behind her, his hands brushing her hips every so often. Everything about the moment replicated *that* dance eight years ago. The alcohol rushed to her head, weakening the bonds of her control. The heat from his body drew her in, forcing her to him as if by magnetic force.

'I always said pretty girls shouldn't have to dance on their own,' he murmured into her ear.

'And *I* always said I would never fall for your cheesy lines.' She turned her head slightly, meaning to give him the brush-off, but his arm snaked around her waist and closed the gap between them. Her butt pressed against his pelvis and she resisted the urge to rock against him. 'Besides, I'm not on my own.'

'I know. You're with me.'

He spun her around and drew her to him. In sneakers, she could almost reach his collarbone with her lips, and she had an urge to kiss the tattoo that peeked out of his top. She was always fascinated by ink. The idea of permanence appealed to her. But life had taught her that everything was fleeting: money, success, love…

'I'm not *with* you, Brodie. You should stop confusing fantasy with reality.'

'It's hard to do when you have all that black make-up on.'

Her cheeks flamed and he laughed, holding her tight. It was all she could do to remain upright. With each knock of his hips, his knees, his thighs, her resolve weakened. Maybe one kiss wouldn't hurt—just so she could see if it was as good as she'd always imagined. Just so she could see if he tasted as amazing as he smelled.

His hand skated around her hip, a finger slipping under the hem of her tank top to trace the line of skin above her shorts. She squeezed her legs together and willed the throbbing to stop. Clearly she had a little pent-up frustration to deal with, but that wasn't an excuse to let Brodie unravel her.

Chantal spun back around and stepped out of his grip. The others had started to drift away. Kate and Scott had retired into the cabin; Amy and Jessica were finishing off the last of the bubbles and sat with their legs dangling over the edge of the boat. Willa was sitting next to them, her phone tucked between her shoulder and her ear.

'What are you going to do now, Little Miss Perfect?' Brodie's lips brushed her ear. 'It's just us.'

His fingertip traced from the base of her ear down her neck, until he plucked at the strap of her tank top. She burned all over with hot, achy, unfulfilled need. The music had been turned down but the bass still rumbled inside her, urging her to swing her hips and brush against him.

'I'm dancing.'

'You're taunting me.'

The unabashed arousal in his voice tore at the last shreds of her sanity, and with each throaty word she came further undone.

It had been so long since she'd been with anyone—so long since she'd experienced any kind of pleasure like this. Just one kiss…just one taste.

She turned, gathering all her energy to say no, but when his hands cupped her face the protest died on her lips. He came down to her with agonising slowness, and rather than crushing his mouth against hers he teased her with a feather-light touch.

'All that teasing isn't nice, is it?'

'I never teased you.' She frowned, but her body cried out for more.

'Back then your every step teased me, Chantal. You were the epitome of wanting what I couldn't have.'

His tongue flicked out against hers, his teeth tugging ever so gently on her lower lip. So close, but not enough. Nowhere near enough.

'You should have got in first.'

His green eyes glinted, the black of his pupils expanding with each heavy breath. 'I thought it wasn't finders keepers?'

'Sometimes you have to take what you want,' she whispered.

So he did.

His lips came down on hers as he thrust his hands into the tangled length of her hair, pulling her into place. She offered no resistance, opening to him as one might offer a gift. His scent invaded her, making her head swim and her knees weaken.

One large hand crept around her waist and crushed her to him. The hard length of his arousal pressed against her. Unable to stop herself, she slipped her hands under his shirt, smoothing up the chiselled flesh beneath. The feel of each stone-like ridge shot fire through her as their tongues melded. His knee nudged her thighs apart and she gasped as though she were about to come on the spot.

What happened to banishing bad choices and focusing on your career? Abs do not give you a free pass.

She jerked back, and the cool night air rushed to fill the void between them. She shook her head, though in response to what she wasn't sure. Her head should have been in the game, focusing on getting her into a proper dance company. Instead she was gallivanting around on a yacht, kissing a man she should have stayed the hell away from the first time.

'I'm sorry. That shouldn't have...' She struggled to catch her breath, emotions tangling the words in her head.

He waved his hand, ever the cool customer. 'Alcohol and sea air—it's a dangerous combination.'

The stood barely a foot apart, unmoving. The muscles corded in his neck as he swallowed, his Adam's apple bobbing, pupils flaring. He might look calm on the outside, but his eyes gave a glimpse to the storm within.

Around them the night was inky and dark. The breeze rolled past them, caressing her skin as he had done moments ago.

'Very dangerous.'

Brodie woke with a start, the feel of Chantal's lips lingering in his consciousness. Had he dreamed it? He rubbed his hands over his face, pushing his hair out of his eyes. White cotton sheets were tangled around his limbs like a python, holding him hostage lest he get out of bed and do something stupid.

Groaning, he sat up and stretched. His mouth was dry and he desperately wanted a shower. The digital clock beside his bed told him it was barely seven-thirty—why was he up at this ungodly hour? He listened to see if a noise had woken him. Were his guests up already? But the only sound that greeted him was the gentle slosh of waves against the boat and the occasional cry of a seagull.

Brodie showered, relishing the cool water on his overheated skin, and then made his way to the kitchen. He didn't drink much coffee, but there was something about being awake before eight in the morning that necessitated a little caffeine.

He fired up the luxurious silver espresso machine; it had been chosen specifically to balance the champagne tastes of the company's clientele with ease of use. Within seconds hot, dark liquid made its way into his cup and he added only the smallest splash of milk before wandering outside.

He stopped at the edge of the cabin, realising he wasn't the only early bird this morning.

Chantal stood in the middle of the deck, balancing on one leg with the other bent outwards, the sole of her foot pressed against her inner thigh, hands above her head. She stayed there for a moment before lowering her foot and bending forward until her hands were flattened to the ground, her butt high in the air. Brodie gulped, unable to tear his eyes away from the fluid movement that looked as though it should have been performed to music.

Flexibility didn't even begin to describe some of the shapes that Chantal could form with her body. Her legs were encased in the tiny black shorts, leaving miles of tanned skin to tempt him. Her hair was free flowing, the dark strands fading into a deep gold at their ends, bleached by hours in the sun.

As if she could sense him she looked up sharply and caught his eye. Unfolding herself, she gave her limbs a shake and made her way over to him.

'Enjoy the show?' A smile twitched on her lips.

'Always.'

She leant forward and breathed in the billowing tendrils of steam from his coffee. 'Got any more of that?'

He motioned for her to follow him and they walked in silence into the cabin. She climbed up onto the chrome and white leather stool at the bench near the kitchenette, her long legs dangling, swinging slightly as she propped her elbows up on the polished benchtop.

'What was that you were doing outside?'

'Yoga,' she said. 'It's part of my stretching routine— keeps me nice and limber.'

'I could see that.' And he had a feeling he would never *un*see it.

'It's good for relaxation too—helps to quieten the mind.' A flicker of emotion passed over her face, but it was gone as instantly as it had appeared. 'Are we all set to sail back to Sydney soon?'

'We sure are. Scott and Kate have plans this afternoon. I promised I'd get them back before lunchtime.' Brodie filled another cup with coffee and handed it to Chantal. 'Are you performing again tonight?'

'No, I have an audition today.' Her face brightened, a hopeful gleam washing over her eyes.

'Oh, yeah. Amy said. In Sydney, right?'

She nodded. 'This is a big one.'

'I'm sure you'll ace it.'

'Let's hope so.'

The doubt in her voice twisted in his chest. Someone with talent like hers should never be in a position to doubt herself, but she seemed less confident than he remembered. Even last night there had been a hesitancy about her that had felt new—as if she'd learned to fear in the eight years since he'd seen her last.

'How come you're not with a dance company at the moment?'

Brodie studied her, and saw the exact moment her mask slid firmly into place as if she'd flicked a switch.

'I'm waiting for the right opportunity. No sense in taking the first thing that comes along if it doesn't tick all the boxes.'

He chuckled. 'You always were one of *those* girls.'

'What's that supposed to mean?'

'You're a check boxes girl. Everything has to fit your criteria or it doesn't even come up on your radar.'

She tipped her nose up at him. 'It's called having standards.'

'It's narrow-minded.' He sipped his coffee, watching as her cheeks coloured. Her lips pursed as she contemplated her response.

'And I suppose you think it's better to drift through life unanchored by responsibility or silly things such as priorities or commitments?'

'You always thought I was such a layabout, didn't you?'

If only she knew what had brought him to the resort in the first place. Most of the kids working there had been on their gap year, looking for a little fun before hunkering down to study at university. He'd been there because he'd devoted himself entirely to taking care of his sister Lydia after a car accident had stolen her ability to walk.

His mother had pushed him to go, and in truth he'd needed the break—needed some space for himself.

'It wasn't just my opinion, Brodie. That's the kind of guy you are—fun-loving and carefree...'

'You underestimate me.' He narrowed his eyes.

'I didn't mean it as an insult.' She sighed and squeezed his hand. 'We're different people, that's all.'

He swallowed. Whatever they had in common, beneath the surface she would never see him as anyone but Brodie the lazy, talk-his-way-into-anything kid at heart. Would she?

'What are you doing for the rest of the weekend?' he asked, an idea forming. 'Do you have to go back to the bar?'

'Not until Sunday. I think they save the Saturday spot for top-billing dancers.' She rolled her eyes, as if trying to hide her embarrassment that he'd brought up her crappy job. 'I was going to hang around in the accommodation there...work on a new routine. That kind of thing.'

'Stay on the yacht with me. The gang will be back to-night and we can hang out some more.' He smiled. 'This would be better than the bar's accommodation. And safer.'

'I don't know if that's a good idea...' She sucked on her lower lip, her eyes downcast. 'I need to focus on dancing right now.'

'Well, you hardly need practice in that department. I've seen you move.' He reached out and grabbed her hand, wanting to soothe the doubt from her mind. 'Stay tonight, and if you're sick of me by the morning then I'll take you back. No hard feelings.'

'No hard feelings?' She looked up at him through curl-ing lashes.

'None whatsoever.'

'Okay.' She nodded. 'I'll stay.'

CHAPTER FOUR

ONCE THEY WERE back in Sydney, and the rest of group had gone their separate ways, Chantal couldn't help but notice how alone she and Brodie were. Nervous energy crackled through her body, lighting up all her senses as though she were experiencing adrenaline for the first time.

It wasn't good. She needed to be calm for her audition—she *couldn't* stuff it up. If she did then she was fast running out of dance companies and productions to approach. What if she couldn't find a real job? Would she be stuck working a pole like those other women at the bar? No, she wouldn't let that happen.

She needed to focus on herself—*just* herself—no messy emotional entanglements, no betrayal, no disappointment. Just her and the stage.

Closing her eyes, she drew a long breath and held it for a moment before letting the air whoosh out. *Breathe in, hold, breathe out. Repeat.*

Staying on the yacht with Brodie was a terrible idea—she needed *all* her focus right now. And Brodie was the kind of guy who could take a woman's sanity and blow it to smithereens with a single look. He'd done it at Weeping Reef, he'd done it last night, and he would do it again.

But that kiss…

Chantal's body tingled at the memory. Brodie's kiss had been exactly what she'd thought kissing would be like as a teenager, before the reality of one too many slobbery guys had shattered the fantasy. Brodie had the kind of kiss that could make a girl's bones melt.

That's because he's had a lot of practice.

'What's with the frown?'

Brodie's voice cut through Chantal's musings. He stood above her, holding out a hand to help her up from her Lotus Position.

A pair of faded jeans hugged his strong legs and a soft white T-shirt skimmed over the muscles in his shoulders and chest. A leather cuff encircled his right wrist—it looked as though he'd worn it for years. The leather was faded and smooth, and it accentuated the muscles in his arm. But Chantal's eyes were drawn to the anchor tattoo on the inside of his forearm, as always. She had to resist the urge to reach out and trace it with her fingertip.

'Where are we going?' he asked.

'Huh?'

'Your audition. Where is it?'

'Right over there,' Chantal said, pointing across the Sydney Harbour Bridge. 'It's about ten minutes on foot.'

'Great—let's go.' Brodie turned and made his way off the yacht.

'You don't need to come with me.'

She grabbed her bag and scrambled after him, her blood pressure shooting up. Having him watch her last night had been humiliating enough. The last thing she needed was for him to witness a more serious rejection today!

'Don't you want a little moral support?'

'No.' She hitched her dancing bag higher on her shoulder and looked Brodie squarely in the eye. 'I've been doing this on my own for quite a while. I like it that way.'

'What if I want to watch?'

He said it in such a way that Chantal almost lost her footing on the jetty.

'You only get to watch when I say so.'

Her blood pulsed hot and fast, flooding her centre with an uncomfortable and entirely distracting throbbing sensation. She didn't have time to be horny. She had an audition to nail and he was getting in her way.

'Brodie, I don't have time to argue.' She waved him off. 'Can't I just meet you afterwards?'

'If you insist.' He shrugged and fell into step with her.

The sun beat down on Chantal's bare shoulders, making her skin sizzle on the outside as much as Brodie was making her sizzle on the inside. Humid air made her skin glisten and frizzed her hair. She yanked the length behind her head and fastened it with a hair tie… Anything to keep her hands busy.

They walked past other yachts, most of them matching the size of Brodie's boat. It was definitely more upscale than the place where they'd been docked last night. A family to their right boarded a boat that looked twice as big as the house Chantal had grown up in. The mother and daughter had identical long blond ponytails and carried matching designer bags.

'Do your clientele look like that?' She nodded towards the family.

'Rich?' Brodie gave them a cursory glance and shrugged. 'Yeah, I guess. People who charter a private yacht tend to have money.'

'More money than sense,' she muttered under her breath.

'It's certainly not the kind of life I had growing up, that's for sure.'

Chantal's curiosity was piqued. Brodie hadn't shared too much about his family while they'd all lived on the Whitsundays. She'd seen a picture of him with a group of younger girls whom she'd presumed to be his family. It had been pinned up on the wall in the room he'd shared with Scott. But other than that she knew little about his family, or where he was from…

'I always got the impression you were well off.'

'Why did you think that?'

She shrugged. 'I don't know… You always seemed so relaxed—so…at peace with the world. It seemed like you'd had an easy life.'

Brodie's blond brows crinkled and they walked in silence for a few minutes. Had she hurt his feelings? She hadn't intended it, but he seemed to lack the tough outer shell of someone who'd struggled their whole lives failing to keep up with everybody else. Someone like her.

'We had our ups and downs,' he said, talking slowly, as though he chose each word with care. 'My family wasn't different to anyone else's.'

'You never talked about your family much while we were working together.'

'You and I never had a serious conversation about anything.' He grinned. 'Too busy playing cat and mouse.'

'We did *not* play cat and mouse.' She shook her head, but her cheeks filled with roaring heat.

'You don't think so? I used to do anything to rile you up, to get your attention. I'd drive you crazy by teasing you about being a stuck-up ballerina.'

'And I'd try to correct you by explaining the difference between ballet and contemporary dance. But I don't think that's a game of cat and mouse.'

'Why do you think I teased you?'

They hovered under the expressway, enjoying the cool reprieve of the shade while people milled around. Sunlight sparkled on the water and laughter floated up into the air as the crowd filtered past. Everywhere people soaked up the rays, ate ice cream and held hands. The Sydney Harbour Bridge stretched out above, the Opera House in the distance, with the sun coating everything in a golden gleam.

Chantal had to admit it. As much as she found the hustle and bustle of a big city overwhelming, Sydney *was* beautiful.

'I thought you were hot.' He slung an arm around her shoulder.

'You shouldn't have thought that.'

He leant down until his lips were close to her ear. 'I *still* think you're hot.'

Caring about his opinion was a mistake, but his words made something flutter low down in her belly. She'd never wanted to be attracted to Brodie, but he had this *thing* about him. It was indescribable, intangible, invisible... but it was there.

She said, 'I think you're full of crap.'

He threw his head back and laughed. 'Prickly as ever, Chantal. Good to see some things don't change.'

'I have to get to my audition.'

She shrugged off his arm and strode in the direction of the Harbour Dance Company's building at the other end of the wharf.

You cannot stuff this up. Focus, focus, focus.

As much as she hated to admit it to herself—and she would *never* admit it to another living soul—Brodie rattled her. He was the only person who could knock her off course with such effortless efficiency. She needed a little distance from him, and tonight she would ask him to take her back to the bar. The feelings he evoked were confusing, confrontational, and she didn't have time for them.

Not now, not ever.

Perhaps if Chantal wasn't so hot when she was mad he wouldn't be tempted to tease her all the time. He loved it when she got all pink cheeked and pursed lipped. Eight years hadn't dulled or lengthened her fuse—she still lit up like a firecracker when he baited her. Hot *damn* if he didn't love it.

Up ahead, he saw her stride quicken, her full ponytail flicking with each step like the tail of an agitated cat. In all his years, through all the women he'd taken to bed, he'd never found a girl who got his pulse racing the way she did.

But he had to get it out of his head—had to get *her* out of his head. Sex with friends was a no-go zone. Normally he had enough choice that steering clear of any women he wanted to keep in his life was a piece of cake. Normally he could resist temptation... But Chantal was testing his limits.

Falling into a jog, he caught up with her. She counted the pier numbers, her gaze scanning the buildings until a soft, 'Aha!' left her lips.

'I'll be in there, but you really don't need to wait,' she said. 'I'm quite equipped to manage this on my own.'

'I've got nowhere else to be. Besides, I might spy a few hot dancers while I wait around for you.'

'Don't forget to leave a sock on the door if you get lucky,' she quipped.

Her eyes flicked over his face, her lips set into a hard line. Was it his imagination or was there a note of jealousy in her voice? *Wishful thinking.*

'You're the only one coming home with me.'

She licked her lips, the sudden dart of her tongue catching him by surprise. He hardened, the ache for her strong and familiar as ever. How was it that she could reduce him to a hormone-riddled teenage boy with the simplest of actions?

He *had* to get it out of his system—otherwise she'd haunt him forever.

'I'm coming back to the yacht with you—not coming home with you. Those two things are quite different.'

'They don't have to be different.'

'Brodie…'

Her voice warned him, as it had done in the past. *Stay away, hands off, do not get any closer.*

'Fine.' He leant down and planted a kiss on her forehead, enjoying the way she sucked in a breath. 'Good luck. I know you'll kill it.'

'Don't jinx me.' She mustered a smile and then turned towards the building marked 'Harbour Dance Company'.

He hated to see her doubt herself. She had no cause to. If the people holding the audition couldn't see her talent then they were blind. Perhaps he should follow her, just in case they needed convincing…

No. She was not his responsibility. He would wait for her, but he wouldn't get involved. He wouldn't get invested.

Brodie settled in to the café on the ground floor of the building, ordered a drink and set up at a small table by the window. Views of the pier with a backdrop of the bridge filled it. Sydney always made him feel small, but in a good way. As if he was only a tiny fleck on the face of the earth and his actions didn't matter so much in the scheme of things. As if he could be anyone he wanted to be…could sail away and no one would notice.

He envied Chantal and the freedom she had. She was beholden to no one. He, on the other hand, was stuck in the constant clashing of his desire to be his own person and his obligation to his family. He would *always* look after his sisters, but sometimes he wanted a break without feeling as though he were abandoning them. Even holidaying in Sydney was tough. What if something happened with Lydia while he was away? What if she got stuck in the house on her own and couldn't call for help?

He shoved aside the worry and reached for a newspaper, making sure to offer a charming smile to the waitress as she set down his coffee. She was cute—early twenties, blonde. But he didn't feel the usual zing of excitement when she smiled back, lingering before heading to her station. Something was definitely amiss.

Several articles and a sports section later Brodie looked up. He'd downed his coffee and then switched to green tea—which tasted like crap—and a bottle of water. A beer would have hit the spot, but he'd skipped training that morning and tomorrow's session would be hell if he didn't get his act together. Ah, discipline…it was kind of overrated.

Chantal still hadn't returned. How long had it been? Time had ticked by reluctantly, but she must have been gone an hour…maybe two. Was that a good sign? He hoped so.

The phone vibrating on the café table pulled his attention away from thoughts of Chantal. A photo of his youngest sister, Ellen, flashed up on screen. She looked so much like him. Shaggy blond hair that couldn't be controlled, light green eyes, and skin that tanned at the mere mention of sun.

'Ellie-pie, what's happening?'

'Not much.' She sighed—the universal signal that there *was*, in fact, something happening. 'Boy stuff.'

'You know how I deal with that.' Brodie frowned.

Trouble related to boys was squarely *not* in the realm of brotherly duties. Unless, of course, the solution to said boy problem involved him putting the fear of God into whichever pimply-faced rat had upset his little sister.

'Yeah, I know. I wasn't calling about that.' Pause. 'When are you coming home?'

'I only left a couple of days ago.' Not that it stopped the guilt from churning.

'I know.' She sighed again. 'Hey, can I come and stay with you when you get back?'

He smiled. 'Are the twins driving you crazy again?'

'No. Lydia's being difficult today.'

The relationship between his oldest and youngest sister had always been tense. And Lydia's mood changes seemed to affect Ellen more than anyone; she was often the one at home, taking on the role of parent when Brodie and their mother were working and the twins were out living their lives.

It might have been easier with another parental figure around, but his dad was best described as an 'absentee parent'. Even before the divorce his father had shunned responsibility, favouring activities that allowed him to 'find his creativity' over supporting his kids or his wife.

'Lydia can't help it. Her situation is tough—you know that.'

'You *always* take her side,' Ellen whined.

'No, I don't.' He sighed, pressing his fingers to his temple.

'You do—just like everyone else!' The wobble in her voice signalled that tears were imminent.

'I'm not taking sides, Ellen, and I understand you cop the brunt of it.'

That seemed to appease her. 'I want to get out of the house for a bit. And I can't go to Jamie's… We broke up.'

Oh, boy. 'Do I need to pay him a visit?'

'No. It was mutual. We weren't ready to settle down with one another.'

Not surprising—she was only nineteen. Brodie rolled his eyes. 'I'll call you when I get home. Then you can come and crash for the weekend.'

Chantal had arrived at the table, and a soft smile tugged at her lips. Was that because she'd had good news, or because she'd caught him playing big brother? He finished up his call with Ellen and shoved the phone into his pocket.

'You're still here.'

Her voice broke through the ambient noise of the café.

'Of course I'm still here. I said I would be.'

She hovered by the edge of the table, hands twisting in front of her.

'You don't need an invitation,' he said, but he stood anyway and drew back the seat next to him so she could sit down. 'How did it go?'

'I don't know. It felt good.' She shook her head and sat, tucking her feet up underneath her. 'But that doesn't always mean anything. They said they'll get back to me.'

'I'm sure you were amazing.' He reached out and grabbed her hand, giving it a soft squeeze.

'*Amazing* doesn't always cut it.'

'It doesn't?'

'No. You can't just be a great dancer—you have to look right, have the right style...' Her cheeks were stained pink and she rubbed her hands over her face. 'These are the big guns too. They didn't even open up for auditions last year.'

Her breath came out irregular—too fast, too shallow. He could see her mind whirring behind those beautiful soulful eyes. He could see the doubt painted across her face. He could imagine the words she didn't say aloud. *I hope it was enough. I hope I was enough.*

Instead she said, 'Some days I wonder if it's worth it.'

'Of course it's worth it.'

How could she say something like that? People would kill for her talent.

'Easy for you to say—you're not the one up there, putting yourself out for every man and his dog to judge you.'

'People judge each other every day,' Brodie pointed out. 'You don't need a stage for that.'

She smiled, her shoulders relaxing as she loosened her hair. The dark strands fell around her shoulders, golden ends glinting in the sun streaming through the café's window. 'Is that a dig at me?'

'It might be.'

He flagged down a waitress and ordered Chantal a coffee. They watched each other for a moment like two dogs circling. Wary. Charged.

'Because I think you lead a charmed life?'

'Because you don't think I work for it.' He took a long swig from his water bottle. 'I do.'

'I know you work for it. But you have to admit you seem to land on your feet, no matter what.'

'And you don't?' He raked a hand through his hair.

'No, I don't.'

She let out a hollow laugh and the sound made him want to pull her tight against him.

'You have no idea what it's been like the last few years.'

'So tell me?'

Silence. Perhaps she didn't expect him to care. Chantal paused while the waitress set down her coffee. She cradled the cup in her small hands, blowing at the steam.

When she stayed quiet he changed tactic. 'How come you never called?'

'You never called either.'

She sipped her drink and set the cup down on the table. For a moment the view of the pier had her attention, and the tension melted from her face.

'I wasn't exactly keen to share that my career was going down the gurgler. Why else would I have called?'

'Because we're friends, Chantal, despite how it ended.'

'You're right.' She nodded. 'Friends.'

God, he wanted to kiss her. She was sex on legs. Perfection.

'Friends who have the hots for each other.'

'I don't have the hots for you,' she protested, but her cheeks flamed crimson and her gaze locked onto some invisible spot on the ground.

'How about you look me in the eye when you say that?'

'Okay—fine. You're kind of a hottie.' Red, redder, reddest. She still didn't look up. 'But you're not my type.'

'What's your type?'

'Tall, dark and handsome?' she quipped with a wave of her hand. '*No* guys are my type at the moment. I have this little thing called a career that needs saving.'

'It's not that you don't have time for guys—you just don't have time for relationships.' Brodie rolled the idea around in his head. 'Maybe what you need is a little no-strings tension-reliever.'

'Is *that* what the kids are calling it these days?' She raised a brow at him and traced the edge of her coffee cup with a fingertip.

'Doesn't matter what it's called so long as it feels good.'

'I'm not a hedonist like you, Brodie. There are more important things in life than pleasure. I need my focus at the moment.'

'Perhaps… But don't you think you could do with a little pleasure right now?'

He reached out and cupped the side of her face. Their knees touched under the table and he could feel the heat radiating from her.

Her dark lashes fluttered. He wasn't going to kiss her again—not yet. She'd run scared if he pushed too hard too soon… But he would draw her in. Relax her boundaries. Give her space to let her guard drop.

Then he would have her.

CHAPTER FIVE

LATER THAT EVENING Chantal and Brodie wandered around The Rocks. To anyone else they might have looked like two people who'd been together forever. Behind the bridge the sun had set, streaking the sky with rich shades of gold, pink and red. Sydney was ready for a night out, glittering and looking its absolute best in the balmy air.

Brodie looked as though he belonged with the glamorous city crowd—as he did with any scene he joined. He had the ability to melt into a group of people no matter who they were. Rich clients, hard-working staff, children—he charmed them all. She'd seen it first hand at Weeping Reef. No wonder he'd done so well with his business.

Women were his forte. He knew exactly what to say to charm them straight out of their panties. Sometimes he could do it without saying a thing. Now she couldn't help but notice the way other women stared at him as they strolled back to the yacht. And why wouldn't they?

His hips rolled in a sensuous, languid gait. He had that loose-limbed, laid-back sexiness that was impossible to fake. You either had it or you didn't. And, *boy*, did he have it!

What is it about focus that you don't understand? Hands off, lips off, eyes off...everything off. Ugh, stop thinking about him!

'You're quiet,' he said as they returned to the boat.

The rest of the Weeping Reef crew would be joining them in an hour or so, and Chantal planned to enjoy her night off. The audition played on her mind, but if she thought about it any more she'd surely go crazy. No, tonight would be an opportunity to let her hair down and relax before she had to go back to the bar.

'My mind isn't,' Chantal muttered.

'Anything in particular bothering you?'

'Just thinking about work stuff.'

It wasn't a total lie, and she wasn't going to encourage him by revealing her inner monologue about his hotness.

'You can't be all work and no play.' He walked to the fridge on deck and pulled out a bottle of champagne, popping the cork and pouring her a glass.

'I think you have enough play for both of us.'

'I'd be happy to share it with you.'

He handed her the flute, her fingers grazing his as she grasped the stem. Goosebumps skittered across her skin and she wondered if perhaps her slinky, skin-tight dress had been a dangerous choice. She'd bought the dress after her audition because it was the exact blue-green of the ocean in the Whitsundays—a fitting choice for catching up with the old gang.

But her arms and legs were exposed to the night air, along with a portion of her back beneath the thick bands of fabric criss-crossing their way down her spine.

It would be fine. The others would arrive soon, and she'd make sure that she and Brodie weren't left alone. Piece of cake.

Yeah, right.

'So what did you do after you left the reef?' she asked, sipping her drink.

'A bit of this and that. There's not much to tell.' He shrugged, dropping down into a seat and stretching his long, muscular legs out in front of him. 'Went to university, dropped out of university, got a job sailing yachts.'

'That's it? Come on—I'm sure a lot more happened in eight years.' She dropped down next to him, resisting the desire to ease against him as he automatically slung his arm along the back of her seat.

'There was a girl.'

'Just one?' she teased, hating herself for the clutch of jealousy deep in her chest.

His eyes darkened, the pale green glowing in the dimming light. 'One relationship. It didn't end well and I don't have any desire to revisit the experience.'

'Why did you break up?' Colour her curious, but she'd never known Brodie to have a relationship with *anyone*. Unless you called repeated booty calls a relationship.

'It was a combination of things.' He shook his head, tilting his gaze up to the darkening sky. 'I was away a lot with work. I had my family to look after. She needed a *lot* of attention. Nothing more than incompatibility, pure and simple.'

'You always struck me as the attentive type.'

'No one is *that* attentive. She wanted us to be joined at the hip.' His voice tightened. 'I don't do inseparability. I need my space—the open waters and all that.'

'How did you meet?'

'She was a friend.' His mouth twisted into a grimace. 'I met her at university but we didn't get together until after I dropped out.'

'I guess she's not a friend any more?'

'No.'

'Sounds like you made the right call.'

'The right call would have been not going there in the first place.' Brodie sighed. 'Some people aren't cut out for relationships.'

It sounded like a warning. Not that she needed it. She

had no intention of getting sucked into Brodie's sex vortex the way other girls did. She knew he was a love 'em and leave 'em kind of guy… It was why she'd stayed away from him in the first place.

But she didn't exactly want a relationship right now either. Didn't that make them perfectly compatible for one night?

Heart thudding against her rib cage, she took a long swig of her champagne. Brodie's arm moved from the seat to her shoulders and his intoxicating coconut-and-sea-air smell made her mouth water.

Would it be so bad to have a little 'no-strings tension-reliever', as he'd called it? Surely she could afford to be unfocused for one day…just a night, really. Not even a whole day.

She was only working at the crappy bar tomorrow, so it wasn't as if she needed to be on her A-game. Maybe it wouldn't hurt. But could she walk away after a single night? Weeping Reef had taught her that Brodie's powers of seduction were second to none. What if he wanted more and she couldn't say no? The last thing she needed was to get sucked into a situation where she had another man trying to overpower her, trying to control her decisions.

She couldn't let that happen.

'What about you? Was it all about the dancing after you left?'

'I stayed a while longer on the resort, actually.'

After watching the Weeping Reef friendships disintegrate she'd wanted to flee. But dance school wouldn't pay for itself and she'd refused to ask her mother for anything else. It had been her time to prove what she was made of. Prove how determined she was.

'But it wasn't the same.'

'We had a great year together, didn't we?'

'We did.'

'I couldn't keep my eyes off you.' His voice was low, rough.

Chantal turned and his arm tightened around her. Her fingers ached to touch him. The now inky sky glittered with city lights. Magical. Surreal. He leant forward, his eyes drinking in every detail.

'Perv,' she said.

Her shaky laugh failed to diffuse the tension.

'I was so jealous of Scott. He had you to himself night after night.'

She tried to shrug his arm away but he held tight. 'And *you* had every other girl on the resort.'

'None of them compared to you, Chantal.' He brushed his lips against her temple, the soft kiss sending electric sensations through her. 'They didn't even come close.'

'Why didn't you say anything?'

She asked it so quietly that she couldn't be sure he'd heard it. Not till his pupils flared and his breath came in short bursts did she dare think about that night. About that *dance*.

'It was wrong being so attracted to you when you were Scott's girl.' Brodie shook his head, blond hair falling about his face.

'Is that why you left?' She reached up and brushed the strands out of his eyes.

His hand caught her wrist, turning it so he could press his lips to the tender skin on the inside. 'Of course it's why I left.'

Breathing was a struggle. Thinking was…impossible. Kissing him was all she could focus on.

'You were *everything*. All I could think about…all I could dream about.' He drew her arm around his neck and leaned in, lips at her ear. 'All I could fantasise about.'

Each word nudged her body temperature higher. Her

hand curled in the length of his hair, gripping, tugging. Resisting.

'Brodie…'

'I've wanted you from the second I saw you at that resort. You were dancing. I'd never seen anyone move like that before.'

'We shouldn't do this…' *Should we?*

His eyes were engulfed by the onyx of his pupils. 'Stay with me tonight.'

'I am staying here.'

'Stay with *me*. In my bed.'

'Brodie…' His name was a warning on her lips, but temptation spiralled out of control. Where was her resolve? Her focus?

'Just for tonight. Then tomorrow we can pretend it never happened.'

He stood and turned, waving to the rest of the Weeping Reef gang as they approached the yacht.

Chantal hadn't heard them. But with Brodie about to kiss her, a bomb might have been dropped and she wouldn't have noticed a damn thing.

'You two looked pretty cosy before,' Scott said.

The boys had separated from the girls and they hung out on the deck, port side. After dancing their feet off— and putting on quite the show—the girls were taking a break in the cabin, a fresh bottle of champagne flowing and peals of laughter piercing the night air.

'No idea what you're talking about, mate.' Brodie put on his best poker face—which, if his track record was anything to go on, was terrible.

'You're so full of it.' Scott laughed.

'You're a bit of an open book, aren't you?' said Rob Hanson, Willa's partner, in his distinctive South African accent. He eyed Brodie with an amused smile that crinkled the corners of his eyes.

Just because Scott and Rob had sorted their love-lives out it didn't given them licence to have a dig at his. Not that he *wanted* a love-life—he was happy with a gratifying and varied sex-life, thank you very much.

'Are you going to get it over with?' Scott took a swig of his beer.

Brodie rolled his eyes and looked out to the water. 'Nothing's going on.'

'Maybe not yet.' Rob smirked. 'But you're better off getting it out of your system.'

Brodie's pocket vibrated and he pulled out his phone. *Saved by the bell!* A text from Jenny—aka twin number one. She'd had a fight with twin number two and wanted a place to crash.

No can do, Jen. I'm in Sydney. Stop giving your sister a hard time.

He toyed with the phone, knowing that there would be an immediate response from his serial-texting younger sister.

'Family?' Scott asked with a knowing look. 'They still driving you crazy?'

'Are they ever?' He shook his head. 'I hope for your sake you and Kate only have boys.'

Brodie's phone vibrated again.

You always take her side.

I do not.

'Is your sister a bit of a handful?' Rob asked.

'Sisters,' Brodie corrected. 'I've got four of them—all younger.'

'Jeez.' Rob let out a low whistle. 'Your parents must have been gluttons for punishment.'

'Not really,' Scott chipped in. 'Brodie always did most of the work with them.'

'Just doing my job.' Brodie waved off the comment. He'd done what any big brother would have. His father's absence had left a gaping hole in his sisters' lives. If he hadn't looked after them who would have?

'Family comes first, but you have to find some balance,' Rob said.

Brodie shrugged. 'The rest of my life is pretty carefree. I sail when I feel like it, work on my business, cruise around the country. Meet lots of interesting people.'

'Brodie has never had any trouble meeting *interesting people*.' Scott rolled his eyes and turned to Rob. 'He used to have the girls falling at his feet when we were all at the reef.'

'It's the tatts,' Brodie replied. 'Something about a little ink makes them go crazy.'

'What's that about tattoos?' Willa wandered over and immediately tucked herself against Rob.

Rob gave her a squeeze and grinned. 'Apparently girls go gaga for Brodie's ink. What do you think, Willa?'

'I don't think it's just the ink,' she said, smirking.

'Should I be getting jealous?' There wasn't a hint of jealousy in Rob's voice, but Willa shook her head anyway. She only had eyes for Rob, anyone could see that.

The rest of the girls had filtered out of the cabin and now joined the discussion. Rob took the opportunity to make Brodie squirm.

'What do you think, Chantal? Tatts or no tatts?' His eyes glittered and he fought back a smile when Brodie shot daggers at him.

'On the right guy it looks good,' she responded carefully, her eyes flicking from Brodie to Rob and back again, as though she were trying to work out who'd instigated the suggestive discussion. 'Though looks aren't everything.'

'Aren't they?' joked Kate, flipping her long red pony-tail over one shoulder as she laughed at Scott's serious face. 'Joking!'

This time the group wasn't crashing on the yacht. Scott and Kate were staying at a hotel for the night, Amy and Jessica were going to continue the festivities at a local bar, and Willa and Rob were retiring back to their newly rented penthouse.

But what about Chantal?

'Are you sure you don't want to join us, Brodie?' Amy asked with a coy smile.

'I would *love* to party it up with you lovely ladies, but I have training tomorrow.' Brodie pulled Amy in for a friendly hug. 'Literally at the crack of dawn—and you know how much I hate mornings.'

She grinned. 'How about you, Chantal?'

Brodie held his breath. This was it. If she stayed then he would do everything in his power to make her come—over and over and over.

She shifted on her strappy tan heels and raked a hand through her long, wavy hair.

'I've got work tomorrow.' She smiled sweetly. 'I think I'm going to need all my energy for it.'

Amy stifled a smile and nodded.

The crew filtered off the boat, leaving Brodie and Chantal completely alone. She hovered by his side, refusing to look up at him. Not that it mattered where she looked, so long as it was his name on her lips.

'I hope you weren't serious about needing energy tomorrow,' he said as they waved the group off. 'You're not getting *any* sleep tonight.'

CHAPTER SIX

Was she making a colossal mistake? Her body seemed to think not. In fact her body acted as though it had been served up a certifiable slice of heaven, complete with whipped cream, cherries *and* sprinkles.

'Sleep is for the weak.'

His hands found her waist and pulled her close. Air rushed from her lungs with the delicious contact. His pelvis was hard against her, the ridge of his burgeoning erection pressing into her belly through the thin material of her dress.

His full lips curved into an impossibly sexy smile. 'I'm glad we're on the same page.'

'We will be if we never speak of this again.'

'Romantic,' he quipped. 'I like it.'

She ran her palms up the front of his chest, feeling the smooth cotton of his shirt glide against her skin. Each muscle in his chest was crisply defined, all hardness and athletic perfection. Her fingers hovered at the top button, tracing the outline in slow, deliberate circles.

'I don't want anything beyond one night. Clear?'

'Crystal.'

Chantal swallowed, Brodie had agreed more readily than she'd expected. But that was the kind of guy he was, the kind of life he led—easygoing, breezy, sans strings. She shouldn't be disappointed.

'Any more rules I should be aware of?' he asked, trailing feather-light kisses from her temple to her jaw.

In heels, she didn't feel quite so small next to him—though he still had a head on her. Perhaps she'd leave the heels on.

A wicked smile curved her lips. 'Ladies first.'

'Hmm…' The throaty growl was hot against her neck. 'A woman after my own heart.'

She thrust her hands into his hair and wrenched his face down to hers, slanting her mouth over his and stripping away any doubts, fears or reservations with a hot, combative kiss. He came back with equal force, his hands sliding down her back until they cupped her behind and forced her against him.

He was hard, salty and heavenly. She moaned, the sound lost between them.

A chorus of cheers and laughter from a neighbouring boat broke them apart.

A giggle bubbled up between her heavy breaths and Chantal pressed her hands to burning cheeks. 'Looks like we're putting on a bit of a show.'

'You *are* a performance artist.'

Brodie lifted her and she instinctively wrapped her legs around him, groaning as her centre made contact with the hard length beneath his jeans.

'But now it's time for a private show.'

He walked them into the cabin, through the lounge and to the bedroom. *His* bedroom. A huge bed dominated the centre of the room. It was a hell of a lot bigger than Chantal had imagined it would be on a boat. It was a bed not made for sleeping but for hot, *Kama Sutra*–referencing, scream-at-the-top-of-your-lungs sex.

Brodie turned and sat on the edge of the bed, still holding her so that she was in his lap. The friction of his jeans against the wispy material of her underwear drove her crazy. She bucked, rolling her hips to increase the pressure. His mouth came down on hers, lush and open and intoxicating.

'Dance for me,' he growled.

Cheeks burning, she pushed hard against his chest so he toppled back. She straddled him, grinding her hips in a slow circular motion. 'But it's so good here.'

'I want to watch you.'

'You only get to watch when I say so.' She echoed her words from earlier in the day, heat flooding her body and throbbing out of control.

His eyes blazed like green fire and darkness. 'I'll make it worth your while.'

'How?' The question escaped her lips before she could think, before she could reason. She needed to hear his answer. Needed to absorb the experience of being with him through her every sense.

Warm palms slid up her thighs, bunching blue material around her waist. His hand brushed her sex, sending a jolt of pleasure through her. Toying with the edge of her underwear, he traced the pattern on the lace with his fingertip.

'If you can walk, talk or function on any level tomorrow then I haven't done my job.'

Her lips trembled. It wasn't enough. She wanted detail. She wanted all of it with a greedy, hedonistic gluttony.

'More.'

'I'm going to take you to the point where you think there's nothing left and I'm going to make you beg.' His eyes were wild, his pulse throbbing in his neck. 'I'm going to make you forget any word you've ever spoken except for my name. I'm going to be the only thing you know. I'm going to be your everything.'

'Brodie…' she whispered, the throbbing between her legs ceaseless. She ached to the point of pain. It had been so long…so very long.

'Dance for me.' His voice was rough, scratched up and torn apart with desire.

She pushed back, balancing on her heels and taking a step away from the bed. Her hands trembled, and her mouth was suddenly devoid of moisture as her hips swayed to a non-existent beat.

She wasn't passionate…her dancing wasn't passionate. Hadn't that been Derek's parting shot as he'd walked out of their house for the last time?

'You're a technical dancer, Chantal, but you're all business. No passion. No one wants to watch that. You'll never make it without me.'

Her throat closed in on itself, her heart jackhammering against her ribs. This was *Brodie*—not her controlling, possessive ex-husband. Smoking hot, life-loving Brodie. She could be herself around him because tomorrow this wouldn't exist. This would never have happened.

Safe in the impermanence of their situation, she ran her hands up her body, over the curve of her bust, the ridges of her collarbones, the column of her neck, into her hair. Fingers divided the strands, shaking her hair out until it fell around her shoulders.

'God, Chantal…' Her name was a strangled plea on his lips. 'Your body is incredible.'

She reached for the hidden zip that ran down the side of her rib cage, drawing it open with agonising slowness. Cool air rushed in, tickling her exposed skin. Stepping closer to him, she pulled him into a sitting position and dragged his hands to her hips so he could feel the movement.

Her head tilted back. There was nothing but the invisible beat and his hands on her. He pulled her between his legs, thrusting the dress up over her hips. His lips made contact with the flat of her belly above the waistband of her black lacy underwear. His tongue flicked out, filled with the promise of what was to come.

She yanked the dress over her head and flung it away.

'Perfection,' he breathed, and the hot air caressed the apex of her thighs.

His hand slid up over her rib cage to clasp her naked breast. Deft fingers toyed with her already hardened nipple, wringing a low moan from the back of her throat.

'Your turn.' She reached for his shirt, unbuttoning him quickly, urgently.

'You're far too good at that,' he chuckled, blackened eyes looking up at her.

'Dance costumes—fiddly buttons are no match for *my* fingers.'

'You do have beautiful fingers.' He pulled one of her hands to his lips and kissed each fingertip in turn. 'Beautiful palms.'

His mouth was hot in the centre of her hand, tracing a line over her wrist and up to her elbow.

'Beautiful everything.'

'Don't distract me.' She pushed the shirt from his shoulders, exposing golden skin stretched tight over a wall of muscle.

The cross tattoo caught her eye. She bent to kiss it, her hands falling to his belt. She wrenched at the closure, making his hips jerk forward as she released the belt.

'Easy, girl.' He covered her hands with his as she lowered the zip.

Within seconds he was completely naked. Ink covered more of his body than she remembered. The cross on his chest had been joined by scrolling words down the side of his rib cage and another anchor lower down, with numbers surrounding it. The sharp V of muscle drew her eyes... then her hands, then her mouth.

Her fingers brushed over the hard length of him, tracing the tip before she sank to her knees and drew him into her mouth. The mixture of earthy masculine scents and the subtle taste of him intoxicated her.

'Didn't I say easy girl?' he moaned, his hands fisting in her hair. She wasn't sure if he meant to hold her in place or pull her away.

She ran her tongue along the length of him before looking up. 'I heard you. I just didn't listen.'

'Come here.'

He hauled her on top of him, tilting them both back so that she straddled his hips. The hard weight of his erection dug into her thigh.

'We've got the whole night. You're not rushing me.'

Stretching his hand back, he found the drawer beside his bed and produced a foil packet. He reached down, sheathed himself, and before she knew what was happening he thrust up into her. The sudden movement was the perfect blend of pleasure and shock...with the tiniest, most delicate hint of pain.

Strong arms held her flat against him, her breasts pushed up against his chest, her lips at his neck. Each moan shot fire through her, and each thrust of his hips bumped her most sensitive part, making her body hum. Orgasm welled within her, climbing, peaking and pushing.

His hands were in her hair again, yanking her face up to his so his lips could slant over hers. Teeth tugged at her mouth, the taste of him drawing her closer and closer to release. She ground against him. So close...so close.

'Come for me, Chantal. I want to feel you shake around me.' His voice was tight, his breath coming in hard bursts.

'Brodie...' Her voice trembled, release a hair's width away.

'Scream for me.'

And she did.

On and on and on she cried out his name, eyes clamped

shut, fists bunched in the pillow, face pressed against his neck. The bubble burst and she tumbled down, down, down. As she clamped around him he found his own release, groaning long and low into her hair.

Silence washed over them. The air was cool on their sweat-dampened skin. He held her close, clinging on as if he wanted to stay that way forever. She didn't move in case he let go.

He could officially die a happy man. The gentle weight of her comforted him. One of her legs had wound around his; her foot was tucked against his calf. As her breathing slowed he stroked her hair, breathing in the heady scent of her perfume mingled with perspiration and sex.

Beside his head her hands were still clutching the pillow. Outside, Saturday-night parties raged on, contrasting with inside, where a hazy silence had settled over them.

'That was okay, I guess,' she mumbled against his neck, chuckling when he turned to look her in the eye. 'If you like that kind of thing.'

Glossy dark strands of hair covered half her face and he pushed them aside, drinking in her drugged gaze with satisfaction. Her lips were swollen and parted, her cheeks bright pink. Tracing her lower lip with his thumb, he brought her head down for a slow, teasing kiss.

'And *do* you like that sort of thing?'

'Nah—orgasms are overrated.' She grinned, pushing herself up so she straddled his hips.

The view was pretty damn good from this angle.

'Blasphemy.'

'Total blasphemy.' She planted a kiss on the tip of his nose and traced the lines of his latest tattoo. 'This is new.'

'It's twelve months old.'

'"In the waves of change we find our true direction".'

She read the words that had been etched onto him forever. 'That's beautiful. Why that quote?'

'I thought it made me sound intelligent,' he joked, hiding his sudden vulnerability with a wink.

How did she do that? She had a homing beacon aimed straight for his most sensitive areas...and not the good kind!

She smirked. 'What's the real reason?'

'I felt like I needed a reminder that change is necessary...healthy.' He sighed, and rolled so that she came down and landed on the bed next to him.

He'd meant to move away, but her body immediately curled into his, finding the groove between his arm and his chest. It felt so damn good to have her by his side, to finally be able to wrap his arms around her without the guilt of the past. He only had one night—he might as well let himself enjoy it.

What if one night wasn't enough?

Bookings were piling up. He'd be sailing back to Queensland soon enough to bury himself in work and his family. Even if they did stretch this fiasco on for more than a night his time here had a solid end date. Normally that was what he liked. But he wasn't experiencing his usual sense of relief at their ring-fenced sleeping arrangements.

'Do you think you need to change?'

'Everyone needs to change,' he replied, running a fingertip up and down her arm.

'What do you want to change?'

He laughed, shaking his head. 'What's with the twenty questions? I thought I'd signed on for a night of steamy sex—not the Spanish Inquisition.'

'Is that so?' She reached for him, the brush of her fingertips hardening him. 'What if I'm done?'

'*I'll* say when you're done.'

Rolling on top of her, he mentally thanked the king-size bed for its endless space.

Pinned, she tilted her face up at him, a defiant glint in her eye. 'You're not the boss of me,' she said.

Yeah, right. He had her exactly where he wanted her. Kissing his way down her neck, he sucked on her skin, only stopping to draw a still-hard nipple into his mouth. Her breasts were perfect: smallish, but firm, topped with bronzed peaks that were oh-so-responsive to his touch. She arched, stifling a groan. He licked, nipped, tugged until she let out the heavenly sounds of pleasure.

'That's it,' he murmured against her breast. 'Don't keep that wonderful sound from me. I want to hear you.'

'Bossy boots.' Her head lolled back against the pillow. Her eyes were closed, but a wicked smile curved her lips.

'Damn straight.'

'We were *talking*.' Strong fingers gripped his hair, pulling his head up so she could look down her body at him.

'And now we're not.'

'Why are you so averse to talking?'

'I'm not averse, but I prefer touching you.' To illustrate his point he kissed a trail down to her hip, swirling his tongue over the slightly protruding bone.

'You're such a *guy*.'

With her hands still in his hair he made his way to the juncture of her thighs, blowing cool air on her heated skin. 'Want me to stop?'

'What if I say yes?'

Her voice wavered. *Victory.*

'I'll call your bluff.'

Delicate licks drew an anguished moan from her.

'Stop.'

'Okay.' He pulled his head away but she pushed him back into place.

'Damn you.'

He laughed against the inside of her thigh, nipping at the sensitive flesh before moving back to her sex. The honeyed scent of her made his head swim, made him want to ravish her. It wouldn't be right to push her over the edge too quickly. She would have to wait while he had his fill.

He drew the sensitive bud of her clitoris into his mouth, working her, teasing her, tasting her. Smooth legs draped over his shoulders; demanding hands pushed and pulled him into place. Chantal was clear about what she wanted, and that was exactly the way he liked it.

'Brodie…' she gasped. 'For the love of…'

'Want me to stop again?'

'No!' The tension built within her, tremors rippling through her legs. 'Please.'

He bore down, giving her what she wanted until orgasm ripped through her. This time there was no holding back. She cried out so loudly that the neighbouring boats were sure to hear.

He clutched at his drawer, grabbing another condom and burying himself in her, riding the final waves of her release as he lost himself in her pleasure.

CHAPTER SEVEN

CHANTAL AWOKE WRAPPED in Brodie arms. Her face was pushed against his bicep, which was far cosier than it should have been, considering the guy was a rock-hard tower of muscle. His even breathing soothed the thumping of her heart.

From her days at Weeping Reef she knew Brodie was a heavy sleeper. She'd tested it on more than one occasion by sneaking into his room with Scott so they could play pranks on him. Like the time they'd switched the clothes in his drawers for frilly girls' nightclothes, so that he had to wander down to Chantal's room in a pink leopard-print negligee.

Not that he'd been too upset. He'd strutted his stuff as he did every day and the girls had fallen at his feet anyway.

Biting down on her lower lip, Chantal watched his peaceful face. Full lips were curved into a slight smile; thick lashes cast shadows on his cheekbones. His shaggy blond hair managed to look magazine perfect. Damn him.

Flashes of last night came back in a rush of needy, achy feeling. Every part of her body throbbed in a totally satisfied, pleasure-overload kind of way. Brodie was as good in bed as she'd suspected, but there was a tenderness to him that had been a complete surprise. The way he'd stroked her hair, the comforting embrace in the middle of the night, the gentle sweep of his hand along her arm—she hadn't been prepared for that at *all*. If anything it would have been easier if he was cold and impersonal afterwards.

She couldn't do this with him. It had been so much more than scratching an itch. He'd pushed her limits, bringing her to sensual heights she'd never known existed. He'd stirred her curiosity. The words inked on him revealed that he was so much more than the shallow charmer she'd labelled him. How could she look into those beautiful green eyes again without wanting to learn more? To dig deeper?

It was supposed to be about sex.

It is *about sex. You don't owe him anything. You got what you wanted—now move on and focus on your career. Playtime is over.*

Careful not to wake him, Chantal extracted herself from his muscular hold. She slipped out of the bed, holding her breath as her feet touched the polished boards. It was like playing a game of Sleeping Giant—except that the giant was a hunky guy with whom she didn't want to have awkward after-sex conversation.

How was she going to get back to Newcastle for her shift at the job from hell? Cringing, she tiptoed around the room. More importantly, where the hell was her dress? She'd managed to find every single one of Brodie's clothing items from their stripping frenzy, but the little blue dress was nowhere to be seen. Normally she was a leave-nothing-behind kind of girl when it came to her clothes, but the blue dress would have to be sacrificed.

Changing slowly, and as silently as possible, Chantal pulled on the clothes she'd arrived in on the first night, grabbed her phone and slung her overnight bag over one shoulder.

Now she had to make her way to Newcastle without the aid of Brodie's boat or her car—which was still parked at the bar. Simple…*not*. A cab was out of the question, since her wallet was frighteningly lean. Perhaps she could ring one of the girls and beg for a lift?

She bit down on her lip. She hated to ask. What if they already had plans? They probably would, and she would be interrupting. The bed squeaked as Brodie turned in his sleep, spiking her heart rate. She had to get out of there.

Pushing down her discomfort, she made her way off the boat and dialled Willa's number. 'Hey, I know it's early, but I need a favour...'

Within twenty minutes she was in Willa's car and on her way to Newcastle. There would be a price to pay for Willa's generosity in giving up brunch with Rob...and it wasn't going to be monetary.

'So,' Willa began, not bothering to hide the curiosity sparkling all over her face, 'how was he?'

Chantal pretended to study an email on her phone. 'I don't know what you're talking about.'

'Oh, come on! I did *not* miss out on baked ricotta and eggs to have you BS me, Chantal.'

'Nothing happened.'

Willa chuckled. 'Then why is your face the same shade as a tomato?'

'Sunburn?' Chantal offered weakly. 'Okay—fine. I slept with him.'

'Thank you, Captain Obvious. I'd figured that out already.' Willa leant forward to watch the traffic as she merged onto the Bradfield Highway. 'I don't want confirmation—I want *details*.'

Where to begin? Images of last night flashed in front of Chantal's eyes, snippets of sounds, feelings, sensations... Her body reacted as though he were right there in front of her. Damn him!

'It was...satisfying.'

'Just satisfying?' Willa narrowed her eyes at Chantal.

'Either you dish or it's going to be a long walk to New-castle.'

'He was amazing.'

Shaking her head, she willed her heart to stop thumping and her core to stop throbbing. She should be satiated, considering he'd woken her up twice during the night to continue wringing as many orgasms from her as possible.

'I'm sure he's had plenty of practice,' Chantal added, folding her arms across her chest.

'Don't go using that as a way to put distance between you. I can see what you're doing there.'

'I am not.'

'That's one thing I like about you, Chantal. You're a *terrible* liar.'

She huffed. Perhaps she would have been better walking. 'I don't need to put any distance between us because we agreed that it would be a one-night-only thing. Then we'd pretend it had never happened.'

'Gee, that sounds healthy.' Willa rolled her eyes.

'Why not? It's just sex—nothing more.' *I don't need any more, and I don't need him.*

'If it was just sex then why do you need to pretend it didn't happen?'

As much as she hated to admit it, Willa had a point. What was so bad about admitting that she'd had a one-night stand with Brodie?

Even thinking the words set a hard lump in her stomach. She'd been down this path before—men always started out fun, till the over-protectiveness stirred, control followed, and smothering wasn't far behind.

'Well, we don't want to upset Scott…'

'That's not it. Scott is totally head over heels for Kate. She's it for him. So I can guarantee he wouldn't care about you and Brodie hooking up.'

Why *did* she feel so funny about it? Perhaps admitting

it aloud meant it was real, and if it was real then it might happen again.

It's a slippery slope to disaster—remember that.

'Eight years is a long time to harbour feelings for someone. No wonder you're scared.'

'I'm *not* scared.' Chantal's lips pursed. 'And I have most certainly *not* been harbouring feelings for Brodie Mitchell for the last eight years.'

'I think the lady doth protest too much.' Willa stole a quick glance at Chantal, her amusement barely contained in a cheeky smile. 'You know, it *is* okay for you to like people—even annoyingly handsome men like Brodie.'

'I don't like him. I only wanted his body.' Her lip twitched.

Feelings for his body were a little easier to deal with than the possibility of feelings for him as a person. She had to shut this down right now. She did *not* have feelings for Brodie and she most certainly didn't want to start something permanent with him. It was a simple case of primitive, animalistic need. Relationships were not something on her horizon.

But no one had said anything about relationships, had they? Crap, why did it have to be so damn confusing? Head space came at a premium, and she could not afford to waste any spare energy on men, no matter how incredible their hands or mouth were.

'Uh, Chantal? I asked you a question.'

'Did you?' Great—now she'd lost her ability to even sustain basic conversation.

'Yes, I asked if you'd heard back after your audition.'

Sore point number two. 'Not yet. But it was only yesterday. They could take a little while to get back to me.'

'Do you think it went well?'

'Who the hell knows?' She sighed, rubbing her hands over her eyes. 'I can't tell any more.'

'I'm sure you'll land on your feet.' Willa reached over and squeezed her hand.

For a moment Chantal was terrified that she might cry. She hadn't allowed herself to shed any tears over her marriage or her failing career, and she didn't plan on opening the floodgates now. All that emotion was packed down tight. There would be time to cry when she'd secured herself a position with a dance company. For the time being tears were a waste of time and energy.

Thankfully Chantal was able to steer Willa to a safer topic. She was all too happy to talk about how things were going with Rob. Other people's lives were preferable talking points over the tricky, icky state of her career and her unwanted feelings towards Brodie.

Willa dropped Chantal off at the bar's parking lot, and she was almost surprised to find her car was still there. It was too crappy to steal, apparently.

Hitching her overnight bag higher on her shoulder, Chantal made her way around the back of the bar to the staff accommodation. She needed a hot shower, a cup of coffee and a lie down before she even attempted to get herself ready for another night of humiliation.

Her unit was number four. The metal number hung upside down on the door, one of its nails having rusted and fallen out. Holding her breath, she shoved the key into the lock and turned. The room didn't smell quite as bad as the bar, but the stale air still made her recoil as she entered the room.

'Home sweet home,' she muttered, dumping her bag onto the bed. *'Not.'*

The small room was almost entirely filled with an ancient-looking double bed covered in a faded floral quilt. A light flickered overhead, casting an eerie yellow glow over walls that were badly in need of a new paint job. A crack stretched down one wall, partially covered by a photo frame containing a generic scenery print. It was probably the picture that had come with the frame.

A quick peek at the bathroom revealed chipped blue tiles, a shower adorned with a torn plastic curtain and a sink that looked as though it needed a hardcore bleach application.

Chantal dropped down onto the bed and checked her phone. Nothing. What was she expecting? Brodie to be calling? Asking her to come back?

Something dark scuttled across the floor by her feet. Chantal drew her knees up to her chest and wrapped her arms around her legs.

She would not cry. She would *not* cry.

Brodie woke to the sound of his phone vibrating against the nightstand. He stretched, palm smoothing over the space next to him in the bed. The *empty* space.

Grinding a fist into his eyes, he forced the fogginess away. What time was it? He groped for his phone, fumbling with the passcode. It was a text from Scott.

Bro, I thought we were going for a run? Where are you?

Run? It was three o'clock in the afternoon. Crap, how had *that* happened?

Sorry, got caught up. Will have to reschedule.

The bed sheets were tangled around his legs and he caught a brief flash of Chantal's ocean-coloured dress peeking out from underneath his jeans in the corner of the room—a sure sign that the lavish images of losing himself in her body over and over weren't from a dream.

His phone immediately pinged with a new message.

Got caught up with what? Or should I say who?

Ugh. Where was Chantal? His feet hit the ground,
thighs protesting as he stood. Yep, that was a sign of one
hell of a night. He stretched, forcing his arms up overhead
and pressing against the tightness in his muscles. Damn,
he felt good.

He poked his head into the en-suite bathroom. No Chantal there. Padding out to the kitchen, he typed a message
back to Scott.

No comment.

She wasn't in the kitchen either. Why hadn't she woken
him? He wandered out onto the deck to see if she was doing
any of her yoga stuff. Nope, nothing there either.

He raked a hand through his hair, coming back to the
kitchen and flicking the coffee machine on. It whirred,
grinding beans and then flooding the room with its delicious, fresh-brewed coffee scent.

Weak. Not that it takes a genius to figure it out...

Scott had a point. It had been bound to happen between
him and Chantal. Their tension had been through the roof
back then, and eight years hadn't dampened it at all. It had
been a special kind of torture having Chantal back in his
life...even if only for a short period of time.

Last night had been easily the best night of his life. But
only because she was insanely hot and did things with
her mouth that would make the most experienced of men
blush. It was a conquest thing—a very long-awaited notch
on his belt.

Yeah, right.

Okay, so maybe he normally woke up *hoping* the girl

had made a quick exit…if he'd even brought her back to his place. Normally he opted to go to hers, so he had control over a quick getaway.

But something about Chantal's leaving didn't sit well with him. He felt the absence of her keenly—almost as if he wasn't ready for it to be over. Understandable, since he'd been lusting after her for such a long time. He needed a little while longer to get it out of his system. Like forever.

So much for the 'hands off your mates' rule.

Frowning, he plucked his espresso cup from the coffee machine and breathed deeply. Where could she have disappeared to? Surely she hadn't gone back to that crappy bar on her own? His chest clenched, fingers tightening around the china cup.

The thought of her getting back up on that stage, dancing in front of those men… It was enough to unsettle even the most relaxed guy. He sipped the coffee, relishing the rich flavour on his tongue, but it didn't satisfy him as much as usual. After tasting Chantal all other flavours would pale in comparison, of that he was sure.

Perhaps the dance company had called her in for another audition? Not likely, since she'd only auditioned yesterday. She *couldn't* be back at that bar. How would she have got there on her own? Her car had never come back to Sydney.

His phone vibrated again, and he was about to curse Scott's name when Willa's photo flashed up.

'Hello?'

'Hey, Brodes.'

The traffic in the background told him she was calling from the road.

'I wanted to let you know I drove Chantal back to Newcastle.'

Dammit. 'When?'

'I dropped her off about an hour ago—I'm still on my way back. It's a long drive! Thought you might want to

know, since I got the impression she hadn't said anything
to you this morning.'

'She hadn't.'

'I don't like the idea of her staying at that place.'

He let out a sharp breath. 'Neither do I. I wouldn't have
let her go...'

'That's probably why she didn't tell you.' She sighed. 'I
only took her because I knew she'd find her own way if I
said no. I didn't want her hitchhiking or anything like that.'

He swore under his breath. 'She makes me lose my
cool, Willa.'

'She must be the only girl ever.'

He ignored the jibe. 'I'll go get her.'

'Good.'

By the time Brodie had sailed back up the coast, the sun
had dipped low in the sky and his blood had reached boiling point. He wasn't sure what made him angrier: the fact
that she'd left him the morning after or that she'd returned
to a crappy job that was not only beneath her but a possible threat to her safety.

Okay, maybe he was overreacting, but that bar *was*
shady. The guys who hung around it were rough. He could
only imagine what the on-site accommodation looked like.
The thought of one of those men following her after she'd
finished her shift...

His fists clenched. He *had* to get her out of there.

He strode across the car park, ignoring the catcalls from
a group of scantily clad girls leaning against a souped-
up ute with neon lights and chrome rims. Inside, a band
belted out metal music, the screaming vocals grating on
his nerves.

Bypassing the growing crowd, he took the stairs up to
the second floor. Would he be able to grab her before she

performed or would he have to sit through the sweet torture of watching her up on that stage again?

The bass thumped deep in his chest as he climbed the stairs. Chantal wasn't on stage. Instead the crowd was cheering for an older woman wearing sparkling hearts over her nipples. Brodie squinted. Were those *tassels*? The stage was littered with a pair of silk gloves, a feather boa, and something that looked like a giant fan made of peacock feathers. The woman shook her chest, sending the tassels flying in all directions.

Find Chantal now! Otherwise she might be the next one on stage, shaking her tassels.

Two girls who sat at the bar looked as though they might be dancers. Their sparkly make-up, elaborate outfits and styled hair certainly seemed to suggest it.

'Excuse me ladies,' he said, approaching them. 'I'm looking for a friend of mine who dances here.'

'*I* can be your friend who dances here.' The blonde batted her false lashes at him, silver glitter sparkling with each blink.

'We come as a pair.' The redhead chuckled, tossing her hair over one shoulder.

'That's tempting,' he said, turning on a charming smile. 'And I'm sure you're both a lot of fun. But I need to find a girl called Chantal.'

'You can call me whatever you like, sugar.' Red winked, blowing him a kiss from her highly glossed crimson lips.

'Are you her boyfriend?' asked Blonde, tracing a lacquered finger up the length of his shirt. 'Most of the girls here don't stick to one guy. They get too jealous.'

'The guys?'

Blonde nodded. 'They start fights. You're not going to start a fight, are you?'

'I'm a lover, not a fighter.'

He watched the bartender eyeing him. The guy was old,

but his arms were covered in faded prison tattoos. Brodie directed his eyes back to the girls.

'You sure look like a lover.' Red licked her lips. 'A good one, too. But all guys go crazy for the right girl.'

'Chantal is a friend. So, have you seen her?'

'A friend? Right.' Blonde laughed. 'If she was just a friend you wouldn't be here with that puppy love face, looking for her.'

He opened his mouth to argue but snapped it shut. Trying to reason with these two would be a waste of time—time that could be better spent looking for Chantal and getting her the hell out of this hole.

'Thanks for your time, ladies.'

'Good luck, lover boy.' Red chortled as he walked away.

He stood by the bar and scanned the room. Mostly men, a few women who might or might not be dancers, muscle stationed by the stairwell and by an exit on the other side of the stage. That must be where the dancers went backstage.

He was about to attempt to get past the muscle when he spotted Chantal. In denim shorts and a white tank top, she looked dressed for the beach rather than a bar. But her face and hair were made up for the stage. She had a bag over one shoulder. Perhaps she'd already danced?

As she attempted to weave through the crowd someone stopped her. A guy much bigger than her put his hands on her arms and she tried to wriggle out of his grasp. The bouncer looked on with mild amusement, but made no attempt to step in and protect Chantal.

Brodie rushed forward, grabbing her by the arm and yanking her back against him. She yelped in surprise, but relief flooded her face when she realised it was him. She stepped back, standing partially behind him.

'Is there a problem, mate?' The guy towered over Brodie, and he saw a snake tattoo peeking out of the edge of his dark T-shirt.

'Yeah, you had your hands on my girl.' He looked the guy dead in the eye, ready to fight if it came to that.

A wave of guilt washed over him. Was this how Scott had felt that night at Weeping Reef?

He shoved the thought aside and pushed Chantal farther behind him. Nothing mattered now but getting her out safely.

'Maybe you shouldn't be letting her parade around in next to nothing, then.' He leered, exposing an aggressive gap-toothed smile. 'Some of the guys here aren't as easy-going as me.'

Brodie turned, wrapped his arm around Chantal's shoulders and steered her towards the stairs. They moved through the throng of people and he didn't let go of her. Not once.

'What are you doing here?' she asked as they exited the bar. Her brows were narrowed, and her face was streaked with conflicting emotions.

It wasn't dark yet. An orb of gold sat low on the horizon while the inky shades of night bled into the sky. Chantal hovered at the entrance of the bar, her eyes darting from the driveway to the accommodation and back to him. The red neon sign from the bar flickered at odd intervals.

'I'm saving your butt—that's what I'm doing.' He raked a hand through his hair, tremors of adrenaline still running through him. 'I'm giving you a place to stay.'

'I have a place to stay.' The defiance in her voice rang out in the night air, and her fists were balled by her sides.

'And how is it? I'm assuming you came back here after you hauled arse this morning?'

The breeze ruffled her dark hair, sending a few strands into her eyes. She blew them away. 'I did.'

'And?'

She folded her arms across her chest. 'It's serviceable.'

'And you'd take "serviceable" over a luxury yacht? Or would that just be to spite me?'

Why was he even worried? She either wanted to stay or she didn't. They weren't in a relationship. So why was the thought of her staying here alone like a stake through his gut?

Too many years playing big brother—that's all it is.

'I'm not trying to spite you, Brodie.' She sighed. 'But I don't need you following me around playing macho protector.'

'What would have happened if I hadn't been here?' He threw his hands up in the air, the mere thought of anyone harming her sending his instincts into overdrive.

'I would have handled it.'

'Oh, yeah? How?'

She waved a hand at him. 'I can look after myself, Brodie. I've done it without your help for the last eight years.'

'I would have been here the second you asked.'

Her face softened, but she didn't uncross her arms. 'But I didn't ask, did I? That's because I'm fine on my own.'

'It didn't look like you were going to be fine tonight.'

'That's *your* perception.'

How could she not see the danger? Was she actually that blind or was it all a ruse so he'd believe her strong and capable? He *did* think she was strong and capable, but the facts still stood. A huge guy would easily overpower her petite frame, no matter what skills she had. Her refusal to accept his help made him worry more.

'Only an idiot couldn't see the path that you almost went down.'

'Only *this* idiot?' She rolled her eyes, flattening her palm to her chest. 'I'm not a damsel in distress—no matter how much you fantasise about it.'

'You think I fantasise about you being in trouble?' Rage tore through him. If only she knew the fear that had coursed through him when he'd realised where she was today.

She opened her mouth to retort, but changed her mind. 'I don't think that, Brodie. But I want you to understand that this thing between us is just sex. You're not obligated to be my bodyguard.'

The words hit him like a sledge-hammer to his solar plexus. *Just sex.* Of course that was all it was. That was what they'd agreed last night... So why did he feel as if she was tearing something away from him?

'Come back to the boat.' He set a hard stare on her, challenging her. 'For *just sex.*'

'I don't want you coming back into the bar.' She loosened her arms, pursing her lips. Her eyes were blackened and heavy, her lips full. 'You don't need to rescue me.'

'Fine.'

It went against every fibre of his being, but he would have agreed to anything to get her away from the bar at that point. He would deal with the consequences next time he turned up to rescue her—because hell would freeze over before he let her put herself in danger. She could get as mad as she liked.

She eyed him warily. 'Okay, then. Let's go.'

CHAPTER EIGHT

THEY WALKED AROUND the side of the bar to the staff accommodation so she could retrieve her bag. Going back to his boat felt like giving in, which seemed spineless after her great escape that morning. But the guy from the bar *had* shaken her. His disgusting words whispered into her ear along with the sickly scent of cheap whisky and Coke had made her stomach churn. Brodie had showed up at the right time and, though she would *never* admit it, she wasn't quite sure how she would have got herself out of that situation.

But it was a slippery slope from accepting help to being controlled, and she would never go there again.

A pale yellow beam from an outside security light spilled into the tiny motel-like room, causing shadows to stretch and claw at the walls. She wanted to be here about as much as she wanted to stab herself in the eye with a stiletto. But the alternative wasn't exactly peachy. Another night on Brodie's boat...another night of searing temptation and slowly losing her mind.

True to his word, he hadn't mentioned them sleeping together, but the evening was young. Something about the way he watched her pack told her he wasn't here out of friendly concern alone.

'How many more shifts do you have?' he asked, hovering by the door.

He stayed close but didn't touch her. Still, she was fully

aware of the heat and intensity radiating off him. He wore a shirt tonight, soft white cotton with sleeves rolled up to his elbows. A thin strip of leather hung around his neck, weighted with a small silver anchor. A silver watch sat on one wrist, contrasting against his deep tan.

'I've got a month in total,' she replied. 'They're pushing for more, though.'

'You're not going to stay, are you?'

'If I don't find something else I might not have a choice.' She faced away from him, stuffing the few items she'd unpacked back into her overnight bag. 'A girl's gotta eat.'

He frowned. 'There must be something else you could do.'

'Yeah, I could wait tables or work as a checkout chick at a supermarket. No matter how bad this is, it's *still* dancing. It means I haven't given up.'

Slinging her bag over one shoulder, she walked out of the room and slammed the door shut behind her.

Silence. She sensed a begrudging acceptance from him.

'No word on the audition?'

'Not yet.'

Once on the yacht, Chantal stashed her things in the guest room, hoping it signalled to Brodie that she had no intention of sleeping with him again. Incredible as they were together, it was clear she needed to focus on her current situation. She was already taking way too much from Brodie. She couldn't rely on him, his yacht or his money. She'd made this mess—she needed to get herself out of it.

'Why don't you grab a shower and I'll get dinner on the go?' he said, already pulling a frying pan from the kitchenette cupboard.

'Are you trying to tell me I smell?' She smirked, leaning against the breakfast bar.

Soft denim stretched over the most magnificent butt she'd ever laid eyes on as he bent down. He was the perfect shape. Muscular, but not OTT bulky. Broad, masculine, powerful. She swallowed, her mouth dry and scratchy.

'If I thought you smelled I would come right out and say it.' He looked over his shoulder, blond hair falling into his eyes.

He mustn't have shaved this morning. Blond stubble peppered his strong jaw, making the lines look even sharper and more devastating. Golden hair dusted his forearms, and she knew that his chest was mostly bare except for a light smattering around his nipples and the trail from his belly button down. She couldn't get that image out of her head.

'Hurry up—before I drag you there myself.'

He said the words without turning around, and Chantal thanked her lucky stars that he didn't. The words alone were potent enough, without the cheeky smile or glint she knew would be in his eyes.

'Then you'll be in trouble.'

The steam and hot water did nothing to wash away the tension in her limbs, nor the aching between her thighs. Wasn't a shower supposed to be cleansing? The quiet sound of rushing water only gave her time to replay the most delicious parts of last night, and she stepped out onto the tiles feeling more wound up than before.

A mouth-watering scent wafted in the air as she slipped into a loose black dress, and padded barefoot into the kitchen. The table was set for two. Intimate...personal.

Two glasses held white wine the colour of pale gold. White china rimmed in silver sported a faint criss-cross pattern—simple, but undeniably luxurious. A bowl of salad sat in the middle of the table.

'Pan-fried salmon with roasted potatoes and baby carrots.' He brought two plates to the table. 'Not fancy, but it *is* healthy—and pretty darn tasty, if I do say so myself.'

'I didn't know you could cook.'

'I'm a man of many talents, Chantal.' He set the plates down and dropped into the seat across from her. 'I thought you would have figured that out by now.'

She rolled her eyes, cutting into the salmon steak and sighing at the sight of the perfectly cooked fish. 'Does it get annoying, being good at everything?'

'No.' He grinned and speared a potato.

They picked up their glasses and clinked them together. The bell-like sound rang softly in the air. Crystal glasses. *Of course they're crystal—this is a boat for rich people... not people like you.*

Chantal shoved the thought aside and sipped her wine. 'Did you do a lot of cooking at home?'

'I did, actually. I was probably the only fifteen-year-old kid who cooked dinner for the family most nights of the week.'

'Really?'

She couldn't hide her surprise. He hardly seemed like the kind of guy who would be in charge of a household. But the salmon melted on her tongue, and the tangy aromatics of a lemon and ginger marinade danced in sensational delight. He didn't cook in the way most people did, where the food was functional first and foremost. He had talent—a knack for flavour and texture.

'Yep. Mum was a nurse and she often worked afternoons and nights. The cooking was left up to me.'

'What about your dad?'

'He wasn't around.' Brodie frowned. 'Dad was an artist, and he had a lot more passion for painting than he did for his family.'

'That's sad.'

'Yeah... I was fine, but the girls really needed him—especially Lydia. She remembered him more than the twins and Ellen.' He reached for his wine, looking as though he were about to continue the thread of conversation but changing his mind at the last minute. 'What about you? Were you the house chef?'

'I can do the basics. My mum worked long hours too, so I had to fend for myself a fair bit.' She swallowed down the guilt that curled in her stomach whenever she thought about her mother. 'I can do a basic pasta...salads. That kind of thing.'

'What does your mother do?'

'She's a cleaner.' Chantal bit down on her lip, wishing the memories weren't still so vivid. 'I don't think she's ever worked less than two jobs her whole life.'

His eyes softened. Damn him. She didn't want his sympathy.

'What about your dad?'

'He left when I was ten.' She shrugged, stabbing her fork at a lettuce leaf more forcefully than she needed to.

'Siblings?'

'None. Probably sounds strange to someone with such a big family.' *Good—turn the conversation back to him.*

'Yep—four sisters and never a moment of peace.'

She envied the contented smile on his lips. It was obvious his family was important to him. She'd bet they would be close, despite his father's absence. The kind of family who had big, raucous Christmas gatherings and loads of funny traditions. So different from her. They'd been so poor at one point that her mother had wrapped her Christmas present—a Barbie doll from the local second-hand shop—in week-old newspaper. The memory stabbed at her heart, scything through the softest part of her. The part she kept under lock and key.

'It drove me nuts, growing up,' he continued. 'But I became amazingly proficient at hair braids and reading bedtime stories.'

Her stomach churned. 'You'll make a great dad one day.'

A dark shadow passed over his face. The wall dropped

down in front of him so fast and so resolutely that Chantal wondered what she'd said. A sardonic smile twitched the corner of his lips. Okay, so there *were* some things that put Brodie in a bad mood.

'I don't want the white-picket-fence deal.' He drained the rest of his wine and reached for the bottle to empty the remaining contents into his glass. 'Marriage, kids, pets... not for me. I've got enough responsibility now.'

'Cheers to that.' They clinked glasses again.

He quirked a brow. 'But you got married.'

'Just because I did it once it doesn't mean I'll do it again.' Her cheeks burned. '*That* debacle is over for good.'

The wine had loosened her limbs a little, and it seemed her tongue as well. She probably shouldn't have accepted the shot of whisky one of the other dancers had offered her before she went onstage. But she'd so desperately needed Dutch courage to force her back onstage.

'Sounds like there's a story there.'

'Maybe.' She shrugged.

Could she claw back her words? Brodie didn't need to see the ugly bits of her life...especially not after she'd gone to such efforts to hide them. Then again, did it really matter?

'I've seen you naked, remember.' He grinned.

How could she possibly forget?

'No point keeping secrets from me now.'

She took a deep breath and decided to throw caution to the wind. After all, he knew her most devastating secret: that her career had turned to crap. What harm could another failure do if it was out in the open?

'The short version is that I was young, naive and I married the wrong guy.'

'And the full version?'

'I married my agent,' she said, rolling her eyes and

taking another sip of her wine. 'What a bloody cliché. He seemed so worldly, and I was a wide-eyed baby. We met a month after I left Weeping Reef, and he promised he'd make me a star. He did—for a while—but then he started treating me like his student rather than his wife. He wanted everything his way, all the time.'

Brodie held his breath... *Dammit*. If she asked, wild horses wouldn't keep him from finding the dude and teaching him a very painful, very permanent lesson. Fists clenched, he drew in a slow breath.

'I couldn't take it. The constant criticism, the arguing...' Her olive eyes glittered and she shook her head. 'Nothing I did met his expectations—he smothered me. Pushed all my friends away until I could only rely on him. I couldn't forgive that.'

'Good.' The word came out through clenched teeth and Brodie realised his jaw had started to ache. 'A guy like that doesn't deserve your forgiveness. What an arse.'

'Yeah, *major* arse.' Her lips twisted into a grimace. 'We ended up separating, and the divorce went through about six months ago. I've been trying to find work but I keep bombing out.'

'Why do you think that is?'

'I don't know.' She shook her head, despair etched into her face. 'Maybe after being told for so long that I don't work hard enough, that I'm not disciplined enough, I've started to believe it...'

'That's complete crap and you know it.' He gripped the edge of his seat, knuckles white from lack of circulation. How could anyone not see the lengths that she went to in order to achieve her goals? She deserved every success in the world.

She managed a wan smile. 'So there you have it: the failings of the not-so-great Chantal Turner. I can't keep a career and I can't keep a man. I can't even book a god-damn dancing job without getting myself into trouble.'

'It's not your fault,' he ground out. His stomach pitched, and the need to bundle her up in his arms thrashed like a wild beast inside him.

'Oh, but it is.'

She drained another glass of wine. Was that two or three? Not that it mattered. He'd keep her safe on the boat tonight. He'd protect her.

'I've done all these things myself. My judgment—my errors.'

'You *can* ask for help.'

She shook her head, dark locks flicking around her shoulders. 'No. I got myself in trouble—I'll get myself out. Besides, I'd need to trust people. I can't do that.'

Her vulnerability shattered him. She'd worked for everything she had—chased it and made sacrifices for it. It wasn't fair that she was here, feeling as if she'd stuffed everything up. He wanted to erase the pain from her voice, smooth the tension from her limbs and barricade her from the dangers of the world.

'You can't go back to that accommodation.' It wasn't a question, and it wasn't a suggestion.

'I need to stay somewhere, Brodie. I need to find a damn supermarket and cook myself a meal.' She shook her head. 'I need to get my life together.'

He wondered if, in her head, she'd told herself that she couldn't rely on him. But he wanted her to… Against his better judgment, he *wanted* her to lean on him.

'Stay here—at least for now. That will give you time to find something else…something safer.' He grabbed her hand across the table, cursing internally when his blood pulsed hard and hot at the contact. 'I'll keep the boat docked here and you'll be close to the bar. Then we can wander around during the day. Have fun. Pretend life isn't such a pain in the butt.'

A small smile pulled at her lips as she retracted her hand from his grip. 'I don't know...'

'You don't have to trust me.'

Her eyes roamed his face before she shrugged her acceptance. 'So that's days and evenings sorted. What did you have planned for nights?'

He swallowed. It would be easy to come up with a list of things they could do at night, and most of them would make excellent use of her yoga flexibility. Hell, how would he keep his distance after what they'd shared last night? He didn't need things getting messy between them, and he certainly didn't want to do anything that would make him lose her again.

'What *about* nights? We can watch movies, chill out on the deck. Keep it PG-13.'

Totally chivalrous—he was simply being a good friend. Keeping an eye out for her. *Yeah, right.*

She smirked. 'Does PG-13 include kissing?'

'It might.'

'Heavy petting?'

'That sounds like it could lead to something a little more X-rated.'

'I want to know what kind of tricks you might try to pull—what loopholes you might use.'

'If I want something I make it happen. Loopholes or no loopholes.'

'Yes, you certainly do.' Her eyes flashed, pupils widening as she shifted in her seat.

Her foot brushed his leg under the table. Had she done it on purpose? He couldn't read her face—couldn't tell whether her flirtatious tone was meant to bait him or mock him. She pushed her plate away and leant back in her chair.

One bronzed leg crossed over the other and the hem of her dress crept up to reveal precious inches of thigh.

'But you can't blame a girl for trying to protect herself,' she said.

'Why do you think you need to protect yourself around me?'

'To make sure history doesn't repeat itself.' She stretched her arms, dragging the dress farther up her thighs. If she kept up the pace she'd be naked soon, and he'd be on his knees. Not a bad thing, given the way she'd cried his name last night.

Cut it out. You're supposed to be helping her—not plotting her future orgasms.

'No more dancing?'

'You're far too tempting on the dance floor. All the girls at the resort thought so,' she said. Her eyes focused on something distant, something lost in memory. 'You're a magnet for the ladies.'

He hadn't cared too much what the other girls thought of him. Only Chantal's opinion had stuck like a thorn in his side.

'That was then.'

'And it's not the case now?' She threw him a derisive look. 'I see the way women look at you, Brodie.'

'Are you jealous?'

'Hardly.' Her brows narrowed, pink flaring across the apples of her cheeks.

He stood, collected the dishes and carried them to the kitchen. He returned moments later with a tub of ice cream and two spoons. No bowls, which would save some washing up. It was only a bonus that they'd need to sit close to share the tub.

'Anything else off-limits?'

He opened the tub and stuck his spoon in, scooping a

small portion of the salted caramel and macadamia ice cream and shoving it into his mouth.

His eyes shut as the sensations danced on his tongue. Sweet, creamy vanilla ice cream, swirls of sticky, salty caramel, and the crunch of toasted nuts. It was heavenly.

It would taste even better if he was able to eat it off that deliciously flat stomach of hers.

Pleasure sounds came from the back of her throat as her lips wrapped around the other spoon. She dragged it out of her mouth slowly and Brodie salivated watching her. If the ice cream was delicious, then *she* was the dessert of the heavens.

'I might have to make this ice cream off-limits. I don't think I'll be able to stop myself polishing off the whole damn tub.' She sighed and dug her spoon back in. 'But we can't let it go to waste—that wouldn't be right.'

'I'll take you for a run tomorrow morning.'

He sucked another tasty morsel from his spoon, focusing on it rather than on Chantal and how her lips looked as if they were made for every kind of X-rated fantasy he'd ever had.

'That should restore some balance.'

'I don't know if I could keep up with you,' she said, tilting her head and toying with her spoon.

'You can definitely keep up.'

Were they still talking about running? She stabbed the ice cream with her spoon, leaving the silver handle sticking straight up like an antenna.

'Tell me more about your family,' she said. 'And please take that ice cream away before I eat myself into oblivion.'

He grabbed the tub, pulled out her spoon and replaced the lid before wandering into the kitchen with her close on his heels. As she climbed up onto a bar stool at the kitchen bench, her legs not quite touching the ground, he felt walls shoot up around him. *Good.* At least some of his defences remained intact. He'd been sure she'd somehow dismantled them.

'Why the sudden interest in my family?'

'I don't know.' She shrugged. 'I felt like you were a bit of a mystery while we were at the reef...and you *did* say we were friends. I know most of my other friends better than I know you.'

'I think we've had enough talking tonight.' He shut the freezer door a little more forcefully than he needed to.

Images of her naked, bending into those damn yoga positions, trailing her hair across his stomach, all invaded him with equal combative power. He wanted her again... and again and again. But they *were* friends. She'd just confirmed it. Breaking the rule once was excusable—heat of the moment and all that—but twice was playing with fire.

He couldn't afford to entangle himself in another relationship, no matter how temporary. He had his priorities all worked out: build his business, take care of his family. That was it. Simple. Straightforward. Uncomplicated.

Chantal Turner was like an addictive substance, and everyone knew the first hit was the best. He'd had his taste—time to move on. She needed to be put squarely in the friend zone.

'I'm going to bed.' He stretched his arms above his head, not missing the way her eyes lingered on him. 'Got to get up early for that run.'

'Sweet dreams.' She hopped off the bar stool, her face in an unreadable mask, and headed to her room.

'Undoubtedly,' he muttered.

The digital clock in the bedroom mocked her with each hour that passed, its red glow holding sleep at an arm's length. She tossed and turned, twisting the sheets into knots around her limbs. What was wrong with her?

Brodie refused to leave her mind alone. One minute he

was hot for her and sharing things about himself, the next he was done talking and wanted to sleep.

It's a good thing he had the guts to do what you couldn't.

Was it possible that now he'd got what he wanted, she was out of his system? That thought shouldn't have rankled, but it did—and with surprising force. Surely eight years of unrequited sexual tension couldn't be over in one night?

Why should she care?

Shaking her head, she turned over onto her side and huffed. It was clear that she'd become unhinged. Perhaps her inability to find a real job was slowly driving her insane, making her more sensitive to things that should have meant nothing. Only Brodie didn't mean nothing…did he?

The bedroom suddenly felt too confined, too tight for her to breathe. Chantal swung her legs out of the bed and stood, relishing the feeling of the smooth floorboards on her bare soles.

She padded out to the deck and tipped her face up, her breath catching at the sight of the full, ripe moon hanging in a cloudless sky dotted with stars. In Sydney the city lights illuminated everything twenty-four-seven and the stars weren't visible. She'd missed them.

Growing up in a small coastal town had meant night after night of sparkling sky—endless opportunities to place a wish on the first one that winked at her. Perhaps that was why everything was falling to pieces now? It had been a long time since she'd made a wish. She closed her eyes, but her mind couldn't seem to form a coherent thought. She knew what she wanted to wish for…didn't she? Her stomach twisted itself into a knot and her breath shortened to shallow puffs.

What if things didn't turn around? What if the dive bar was her best option? *Don't think like that, you* have *to be positive. You have to keep trying…try harder!*

Alone, she felt tears prickle her eyes. The sadness was pushing its way to the surface, mingling with her ever-present panic like blood curling in water. She needed to hang on a little while longer—long enough to get something—*anything*—which would prove she hadn't wasted her mother's sacrifices and her own hard work. Then she could deal with the bad stuff.

'What are you doing up?'

Brodie's sleep-roughened voice caught her off guard. She whirled around, blinking back the tears and pleading with herself to calm down. She didn't want him to see her like this—not when she felt she was about to fall apart at the seams.

'Are you okay?'

She nodded, unable to speak for fear that releasing words might open the floodgates of all she held back. Her breathing was so shallow and fast that the world tilted at her feet. She pressed a palm to her cheek, mentally willing him to leave her. Her face was as warm as if she'd spent the night sleeping next to an open fire, and her skin prickled uncomfortably.

'You don't look okay.' He stepped closer and captured her face in his hands, studying her with his emerald eyes.

That only made it worse. By now her palms were slick with perspiration and her stomach swished like the ocean during a storm. Tremors racked her hands and her dignity was slipping away faster than she could control it. She was drowning, and once again she was relying on him to save her.

'Hey, it's all right,' he soothed, moving his hands to her shoulders and rubbing slowly up and down her arms. 'Let's get you a glass of water.'

He pulled her against his side, wrapping an arm around her shoulder and guiding her into the cabin. Setting her down on a stool, he grabbed a glass and pressed it against the ice machine on the fridge. Loud clinking noises filled the room as the ice tumbled into the glass, followed by the glug of water from a bottle in the fridge.

Breathe in—one, two, three. Out—one, two, three.

'Drink it slowly—don't gulp.' He handed her the glass and smoothed her hair back from her face.

No doubt she looked like a crazy person, huffing and puffing like the wolf from that nursery rhyme. Her hair would be all over the place, sticking out like a mad professor's. It was only then she realised that she was practically naked, with a pair of white lace panties her only keeper of modesty. She hadn't thought it possible for her face to get any hotter, but it did.

'Thanks,' she mumbled, shaking her hair so it fell in front of her, covering her bare breasts.

She must have ditched her T-shirt while she was trying to get to sleep. Stress overheated her. Most of the time she slept in nothing at all—unless it was the dead of winter, and then she wore her favourite llama-print pyjamas. But it was warm on the boat and her body was reaching boiling point. She pressed the cool glass to her burning cheek.

You're rambling in your head—not a good sign. Calm. Down. Now.

'Do you want me to grab you something to wear?'

Brodie's voice cut into her inner monologue and she nodded mutely, switching the glass of water to her other cheek. Her whole body flamed. Shame tended to do that. This was exactly why she should have said no to the invitation to Brodie's boat in the first place! Now he knew... He knew what a mess she was. She couldn't even fall asleep without working herself up.

'Here.'

He took the glass from her hand and set it down, helping her weakened limbs into the armholes of a T-shirt and guiding her head through the neck opening.

The fabric swam on her, smoothing over her curves and giving her protection. The T-shirt was his—it smelled of him. Smelled of ocean air and soap and earthy maleness.

'Are these panic attacks a recent thing?' He leant against the bench, his face neutral.

'No, I've had them a while.' She couldn't look him in the eye.

'They suck,' he said. 'My little sister gets them pretty bad too. Water usually works for her.'

Chantal bit down on her lip, toying with the glass before taking another sip. Could she be any more humiliated right now?

'It's nothing to be ashamed of. You know that, right?'

He touched her arm, the gentle brush making her stomach flip. Her breathing slowed a little.

'Ellen gets them a lot. She's only nineteen, but she puts a lot of pressure on herself to do well. She wants to get into a performing arts school.'

'What does she do?' Curiosity piqued, she looked up.

Brodie dropped down onto the stool next to her, his knees inches from her thighs. 'She plays piano pretty damn well, if I do say so myself. I used to run her to practise when I lived at home—went to all her recitals too. She's ace.'

The pride in his voice was unmistakable. Chantal had often wondered what it would be like to have siblings—to look after someone other than herself, to worry about people all the time. She would have been a terrible sister—she couldn't even keep her own life together, let alone help anyone else.

'Then there's the twins: Jenny and Adriana. They're twenty-two, and as diffcrent as two people can be. Jenny is the loud one. She got into modelling a while ago and has done a fair bit of travelling with it. Adriana is still studying. She's going to end up being a doctor of some-

thing one day.' He smiled. 'Then Lydia is the oldest…
she's twenty-four.'

His eyes darkened for a moment and she wondered if
he was going to continue. His lips pulled into a flat line
as he raked a hand through his hair, stopping to rub the
back of his neck.

'Lydia is in a wheelchair. She was in a car accident some
years ago and she was paralysed from the waist down.'

'That's awful.'

'Yeah.' A sad smiled passed over his lips. 'She wanted
to be a dancer.'

Emotion ran through her—grief for this poor girl whom
she didn't even know, for the sadness on Brodie's face and
for what their family must have gone through. At least she
could still dance. Her heart swelled. He cared so deeply
about his family. For all her jokes about his carefree attitude, he was a good person.

He drew a breath, steadying his gaze on her. 'So there
you go. You wanted to know something else about my
family—it's not all sunshine and roses.'

'I guess we've all got our stuff to deal with.' She downed
the rest of her water. 'I nearly gave up dancing once.'

'Really?' His blond brows arched.

'It wasn't long after my dad left. We didn't have a lot
of money and Mum had lost her job cleaning one of the
local motels.' The memory flowed through her, singeing
her heart with the same scorching hurt that came every
time she remembered what life had been like back then.
'She picked up cleaning work at my school. The kids used
to tease me, so I told her that I wanted her to find another
job…but there aren't a lot of jobs in little beach towns.'

Why was she telling him this? She hadn't told *anyone*
this story—not because she was ashamed of having grown
up with no money, but because she'd been so horrible to

her mother. More than a decade and a half later, guilt over her behaviour lingered.

'She gave me a choice. Give up dancing and she would quit her job at the school—because that's what it was paying for. Otherwise, if I wanted to keep dancing, she had to keep working two jobs.' She squeezed her eyes shut for a moment. 'So I gave up dancing for a week.'

'You can't blame yourself that. How old were you? Ten? You were just a kid.'

'I don't think I've ever hurt her as much as I did then.' She shook her head, amazed that it felt as though a weight had been lifted from her shoulders. 'I wish I could take it back.'

'I'm sure she knows how you feel.'

'I hope so. She gave up so much for me to be able to continue dancing. She hardly ever came to my competitions or exams because she was always working, but she never complained.' She let out a hollow laugh. 'Not once.'

'She never gave up?'

'Nope.' She shook her head. 'Which means *I* can't give up.'

'Sounds like you got a lot of your tenacity from her.'

The tenderness in his voice sparked her insides, lighting up her whole body—as if he had a direct 'on' switch to her nervous system. Her hands were fluttering in her lap. The desire to reach out and touch him made her fingers tingle. If she didn't put some distance between them—and fast—she'd do something stupid.

'Thanks for the drink.'

She went to hop off her stool but Brodie's hand came down on her bare thigh. His fingers skimmed over her knee, touching the hem of the T-shirt. The touch was so light she could easily convince herself that she was imagining things. Despite her brain shouting out warnings, she didn't want this to be a dream.

'Is it wrong that I couldn't sleep because I was thinking about you?' he asked.

His bare torso was the only thing she could look at. Broad shoulders, the ripple of muscle at his abdomen, the V that dipped below his cotton pyjama bottoms. He would be naked underneath them. She could tell from the inadequate way the thin fabric concealed the length of him.

Her breath hitched, and the sudden flutter of her heart had nothing to do with panic. 'You were the one who wanted to go to sleep.'

His hand inched up, the tips of his fingers slipping under her hem of the T-shirt. Each millimetre his hand travelled stoked the fire low in her belly, stirred the tension in her centre. She pressed her thighs together, rocking gently against the stool in the hope that it would ease the need in her.

It didn't.

Nothing would ease the need except him. He was the only solution to her problem, the only cure for her ailments. In that moment she was raw. Exposing her past had opened up something within her—a cavernous hunger long buried by insecurities and fear. He'd shown her it was safe to be who she was, to open up and allow herself to be vulnerable. She wanted nothing more than to wipe away the old hurt with new pleasures. To erase the parts of herself that clung to bad memories, to be a new person.

'You were the one who wanted to figure out what loopholes I might use to make a move on you,' he said, eyes blackened with desire.

'Have you thought of any yet? Because I could use a loophole right about now.'

CHAPTER NINE

IT WAS ALL the invitation he needed. Willpower was a fragile thing, easily overridden by blazing attraction, pent-up sexual tension, and too many dirty dreams. Could he take her into his bed a second time, knowing that it wasn't going anywhere? Knowing that he wouldn't *let* it go anywhere because his life didn't have room for her?

'Brodie?'

A plump lower lip was being dragged through her teeth, and the desperation in her voice urged the increased thumping of his heart.

Even if he'd wanted to pretend he wasn't interested he didn't have the opportunity. She jumped down from her stool and stood between his legs, her hands finding the rigid muscles in his thighs, brushing the aching hardness of his erection.

'We're friends.' He pushed off his stool and moved into the kitchen, opening the freezer door and pretending to look for something.

'Friends who have the hots for each other.' She echoed his words with a cheeky smile.

The cold of the freezer wasn't making him any less hard or any less horny. In fact it had only drawn his eyes to a chilled bottle of vodka. He wrapped his hand around the neck, savouring the ice-cold glass against his heated palm. A cold shower would have been better, but getting naked might prove dangerous.

'Tell you what,' she said, reaching past him and grabbing the bottle out of his hand. 'If you can drink a shot of this off me and still not want to sleep with me, I'll let you go back to bed.'

He slammed the freezer door shut and turned, resting his back against it. 'You'll *let* me?'

'Yes.' She unscrewed the bottle. 'I'll let you. And I won't mention it in the morning—or ever again.'

'Why are you suddenly trying to seduce me with body shots when before you were more concerned about setting up barriers?' He raked a hand through his hair and tried not to think about how naked she was under his T-shirt.

'Why the psychoanalysis?' She raised a brow. 'Can't a girl change her mind?'

'I have a rule about sleeping with my friends.'

'What happened to that rule last night?' She smirked. 'You didn't seem to be too worried about rules then. Or are you afraid that you won't be able to say no after your little drink?'

She knew how to fire up his competitive streak—and she *did* have a point. He hadn't been all that worried about his rule last night. But the rule existed for a reason. Sleeping with her would be messy in both the best and worst ways. It would mean dealing with the awkward aftermath and potentially losing their friendship if things went pear-shaped. He'd made an exception for Chantal because he'd wanted to get her out of his system, but now he was caught between taking the safe route and taking what he wanted.

That backfired, didn't it? Man up—do the shot and then go to bed.

'Fine.' He grabbed the bottle from her grip and located a shot glass.

As he turned around Chantal was slowly peeling off his

T-shirt. The white lace scrap covering her sex was revealed first, then a flat bronzed plane of stomach, two perfectly formed breasts, collarbones and a long mane of dark hair as she whipped the T-shirt off. He'd need a drink now. His tongue felt dry and heavy in his mouth.

'Ready?' She hoisted herself onto the bench.

'You still have to tell me why the sudden change of heart.' With a shaking hand he poured vodka into the shot glass.

'Maybe I realised that I should be grateful for the things I have, no matter how tough it is right now.' She lay back and stared intently at a spot on the roof, lower lip between her teeth.

He'd got to her with the story about his sister. Though he was hoping she'd apply it more to cutting herself some slack and persisting with her dance career—not to mention leaving that trashy bar—rather than to jumping back into bed with him.

'And you're grateful for having sex with me?'

'I'm grateful for orgasms.' Her head tilted so she could look at him. 'It's been a long time since I let myself have any fun.'

'It *is* fun, isn't it?' He stepped closer, smoothing a hand over her stomach. 'Just a bit of fun—nothing more.'

He poured the vodka into her belly button, the excess liquid spilling out onto her stomach. She let out a sharp cry at the coldness but he dropped his head and sucked, lashing his tongue across her belly and catching the liquid before it spilled onto the bench. It burned for a second, and then a smooth warmth spread through him.

The alcohol mingled with the taste of her warm skin. He ran his tongue down to the edge of her underwear, watching the slick trail he left behind. Her fingers thrust into his hair as he snapped at the waistband with his teeth, a low groan rumbling from deep inside her. He should have pulled away then, but the vodka felt good. It softened his edges, warmed his limbs. It made it easier to forget that sleeping with her was a bad idea.

A tasty, satisfying, *perfect* bad idea.

'Don't worry—I don't expect anything.' Her voice had become rough, husky. 'A bit of fun is exactly what I need. No strings, no obligation.'

'So you're not going to fall for me?'

The scratch of her lace underwear against his tongue sent a shiver through him. He pressed his lips to the peak of her sex and was rewarded with a gasp and the sharp bite of her nails against his scalp.

'You wish.'

Smooth skin beckoned to him. Hooking a finger beneath the waistband, he peeled her underwear down to mid-thigh, trapping her legs and preventing them from opening. His lips found the bare smooth skin of her centre, pressing down with agonising slowness. A quick swipe of his tongue had her hips bucking against him.

'This is cruel…and unusual.' Her hands dug deeper into his hair, wrenching his head up. 'I can't move properly.'

'Anticipation, Chantal. Just go with it.'

He grabbed her wrist and put her hand down by her hip, holding on so she couldn't move. His other hand teased her, his thumb rubbing against the sensitive bud of her clitoris in slow, circular movements. His tongue followed, parting her so he could claim her most sensitive spot between his lips. Her movement was restricted by the underwear holding her prisoner and she writhed against him in unfulfilled need.

'Please…' she panted. Her eyes had rolled back; her mouth was slack with pleasure. Her hair trailed over the side of the bench, brushing against the kitchen cupboards as she moved.

The sight of her laid out like an extravagant dessert

was almost enough to send him over. He wanted to taste every inch of her, keep her begging while he feasted. He released her from her lacy bindings and his fingers found her hot and wet. His mouth came up, capturing a bronzed nipple as she squirmed, grinding again his hand until her cries peaked.

She shouted his name over and over, until the syllables jumbled together into an incoherent decree of passion and release. Shock waves ran through her and he withdrew his hand slowly, gently. His mouth found hers, his tongue parting her lips and bringing her back to the moment.

'Still think I'm cruel?' he murmured against her mouth, sliding a hand beneath her neck to lift her into a sitting position.

She faced him, wrapping her legs around his waist. Heat enveloped him as her hand slid down the front of his pants and stroked his erection. She caressed him—long, slow movements designed to make him want something out of reach.

'I think you've got magic hands,' he said.

Hair tickled his chest as she rested her head against him, still touching him. He pressed into her hand, gasping at the sharp flare of pleasure that forced his eyes shut.

'Brodie?'

Olive eyes met his, the black of her pupils wide. Her tongue swiped along his lower lip, the taste of her tempting him.

'I want you inside me. Now.'

Her hands tugged down his pants, exposing him to the warmth of her thighs. He lifted her from the bench and carried her to the bedroom. They landed on the bed, her body pinned beneath his, and he reached out to his drawer and withdrew a condom. Sheathing himself, he plunged into her. His mouth slanted over hers, hot, demanding. He savoured her heat and tightness until she couldn't hold on.

Her muscles clenched around him—thighs around his waist, arms around his neck. He couldn't hold back, couldn't stop the desire to drown in her warm skin and open mouth. Burying his face against her hair, he brought her close to the edge again. She shook, holding on as if she were about to fly away.

'Let go,' he whispered. 'Just let go.'

And she did. Crying, shaking, gasping. Her orgasm ripped through her with an intensity that brought on his own release within seconds. He rode her slowly, until the waves of pleasure subsided.

The realisation that she wasn't in her own bed came swiftly when morning broke. Sunlight filtered into the room—Brodie's room—and the ache between her thighs confirmed that she hadn't imagined those naughty images of them in his kitchen. It wasn't a dream—it was the mind-bending truth.

Brodie was like peanut butter ice cream with extra fudge. Decadent, tasty, hard to say no to. But, like all delicious things, he wasn't the best choice she could have made. What she needed was a steady diet of apples and focus—not ice cream and orgasms.

'Morning,' he murmured against the back of her neck.

One arm was slung over her mid-section, turned slightly to expose the edge of his anchor tattoo. She traced the outline with her fingertip. Something firm dug into her lower back. She moved under the guise of stretching her back, smiling when he groaned and pressed against her.

'Don't start what you can't finish.'

She chuckled. 'You're insatiable.'

'Says you, Miss Body Shot. I was perfectly happy sleeping on my own last night.'

'Liar.' She rolled over, catching his stubble-coated jaw with her cupped hand.

He didn't hesitate to kiss her, his tongue delving and tangling with hers. A hand found her breast, fingers tugging and teasing her nipple until she gave in and let him roll on top of her.

'Weren't we supposed to be going for a run this morning?' she asked, blinking her eyes at him with faux innocence.

'I know a few other things we can do that will burn calories.'

Apples, not ice cream.

'Worried you won't be able to keep up?'

'Ha!' He grinned. 'Like I said before, don't start what you can't finish.'

'Oh, I can finish it.' She tipped her chin up at him, giving his chest a playful shove. 'Loser makes breakfast.'

'You're on.'

Chantal regretted making the challenge a few ks into the run, when it became clear that Brodie was much better at running than she was. He jogged effortlessly alongside her, breaking into a sprint every so often to prove he could. The Newcastle coast blurred past in a haze of blue skies, bluer waters and pale sand. How was it possible to be in such a beautiful place and not be able to enjoy the scenery?

'Can we take a break?' Chantal slowed to a walk and fanned her face.

'Conceding defeat already?' He jogged on the spot, a victorious grin on his face. 'You know that means you'll be making my scrambled eggs when we get back?'

'Fine. You win.' She waved him away as she took a long swig from her water bottle. 'Looks like dancing fitness doesn't translate to running fitness.'

'No need to make excuses,' he teased, and she elbowed him.

'No need to be a smug winner.'

He reached for her water bottle, tipping it to his lips and

gulping the liquid down. Muscles worked in his neck. It was hard not to stare at how he made the most regular of actions seem inherently male.

'It's not often I get one over you, so let me have my moment. Besides, I've got a long way to go if I'm going to run a half marathon.'

Her brows furrowed. 'You're training for a marathon?'

'*Half* marathon,' he corrected.

'How far is that?'

'Just over twenty-one k.'

'Funny how you didn't tell me that when you let me challenge you to a run.' She narrowed her eyes at him. 'Cheater.'

A booming laugh erupted, startling a woman jogging past with her small dog. 'That's not cheating.'

'Why on earth do you want to run that far?'

He shrugged. 'To see if I can do it. A buddy challenged me, and you know how I am with challenges.'

'It just seems…' She took in the gleam of his tanned skin, the T-shirt that hugged his full biceps, the golden hair on his athletic legs. 'Out of character.'

'Why? Because I don't have the discipline to be a runner?' A bitter tone tainted the words.

'No, I meant because you're more of a water sports kinda guy.' She cocked her head, studying him. 'Windsurfing, sailing boats, water-skiing…that kind of thing.'

'Oh.' A smile tugged at the corner of his lips.

'I always wondered if you were half dolphin, since you spend so much time in the water.'

'Wouldn't that make me a mermaid?'

'Mer*man*,' Chantal corrected, gesturing with her water bottle.

'That's not manly.' He crossed his arms. 'What about half shark?'

'Whatever floats your boat, Mr Cheese.'

Strong hands grabbed her arms and hauled her to him. His mouth came down near her ear. Hot breath sent goosebumps skittering across her skin.

'Looks like you finally fell for my cheesy lines after all.'

Uneasy waves rocked her stomach. She'd certainly fallen for something. Her attraction to Brodie had always been physical...at least that was what she'd told herself. She was attracted to him *in spite* of his joker, take-nothing-seriously personality. At least it had *used* to be in spite of that...

Now she was the one convincing him to pour vodka on her, challenging him to a competition, teasing him about being a merman. This wasn't *her*. She was never this... relaxed.

'I haven't fallen for anything, Brodie. You're just good in bed.'

'Just sex.' His eyes avoided hers and he bent to inspect his shoelaces. 'That's all I was aiming for.'

An awkward silence settled over them. Could the exchange have felt as hollow to him as it did to her? Could he sense the fear in her voice as she tried her hardest to pull a barrier up between them?

'Let's head back,' he said, turning in the direction from which they'd come. 'I'm ready for my winner's breakfast.'

The tinkling of cutlery mingled with the rush of waves on the shoreline below. Tea light candles flickered in the gentle ocean breeze, and the smell of sea air mixed with the mouth-watering smells of steak and freshly cooked seafood.

'What's up?' Scott took a swig of his beer. 'You seem tense.'

Brodie had almost forgotten that Scott and Kate had agreed to make the trek up to Newcastle for a drink that night, at one of the beach hotels run by Brodie's friend.

Once Kate had caught wind that Chantal was staying on the boat she'd insisted they make it a double date of sorts. Having Chantal there meant he couldn't forget their run earlier that day—couldn't stop her comment swirling around in his head, kicking up all the memories and feelings he'd buried long ago.

I haven't fallen for you, Brodie. You're just good in bed.

In no possible situation should that have upset him… but he was off-kilter. Agitation flowed through him like a disruptive current, causing him to drum his fingers at the edge of the table where the group sat. Since when was being good in bed a *bad* thing?

'Maybe all this water is turning your brain to sludge.' Scott gestured towards Brodie's tall glass of mineral water. 'Why don't you have a beer?'

'The race is next week and I've reached my quota of indulgence.' He put on a fake smile and hoped that Scott had consumed enough beers not to look too hard. 'I'm winning that bet.'

The girls had gone to the bar for more refreshments. They stood side by side, giggling and chatting animatedly. Chantal's short black skirt skimmed the backs of her thighs, leaving miles of long tanned legs gleaming in the golden early-evening light. Her shoulders were barely contained in a flowing white top with small gold flowers. A small tug would be all it would take to free her, to expose her breasts to his mouth.

Brodie watched as they fended off an enthusiastic approach from a group of guys who appeared to be on a bucks' night.

'Maybe I should see if the girls need a hand,' Brodie said, frowning.

'She's got to you again, hasn't she?'

'Huh?'

Scott laughed, slapping him hard on the back. 'Oh, man, I didn't realise how bad it was. You get this look on your face when she's around—don't know how I missed it back at the reef.'

'You're full of crap.'

'*You're* an open book.' Scott's fist landed hard on his bicep. 'And when it comes to Chantal—'

'It's just sex.' *Good* sex, according to Chantal, but *just* sex.

'Yeah, and a half marathon is *just* a run.' Scott narrowed his eyes, studying Brodie in that analytical way of his.

'You know me. I don't do relationships. Surf, sand, bikinis—that's what it's all about.'

'Maybe before.' Scott shrugged. 'Doesn't explain why you look like you're about to snap the table in two because some guys are talking to her.'

Brodie looked down. Sure enough, his white-knuckled grip on the table was a little unusual. 'Says you. I thought you were going to deck me that time I danced with Kate.'

'I thought I was too. And why was that, huh?' Scott chuckled. 'Anyway, I'm not letting you get away with changing the subject. You helped me and now it's my turn to help you.'

'I don't need help.' Brodie let go of the table and ran his palms down the front of his jeans.

'You don't want help, but you damn well need it.'

The girls arrived back at the table, champagne in hand, plus a beer for Scott and another mineral water for Brodie.

'How does it feel, being a teetotaller?' Kate asked, flipping her long red hair over one shoulder.

'It's temporary. I don't think I could handle it long-term.' Brodie twisted the cap on his bottle, waiting for the rush of bubbles to die down before removing it. 'But temporarily it's okay. I can handle temporary things.'

Scott kicked him under the table and rolled his eyes. Okay, so maybe subtlety wasn't his strong suit. Nervous energy coursed through him, making the words in his head stumble and trip over one another. Kate eyed him curiously and Chantal pretended to be deeply involved in something on her phone.

Brodie contemplated smoothing things over, but his own phone vibrated against the table. Home.

'Hello?'

'Hey, Brodie.' The voice of his youngest sister, Ellen, came through the line. Her voice was pinched—a sure-fire sign that she was about a hair's breadth away from flipping out about something.

'What's up, Ellie-pie?'

'It's Lydia, she's had a down day. She won't eat her dinner. Mum's at work, but she said I had to make sure Lydia eats.'

The words ran into one another, and the wobble in her voice twisted like a knife in his stomach.

'Where are the twins?'

Sniffle. 'Jenny's at a party and Adriana hasn't come home from uni.'

'Put Lydia on the phone. I'll get her to eat.'

Within moments he'd convinced his sister to have at least a salad, even if she didn't want a full meal. It was hard for all of them to look after Lydia on her down days. There were times when she point-blank refused food and water for hours on end…sometimes days. He remembered a particularly bad patch when she'd ended up so dehydrated he'd had to rush her to the emergency ward. All she'd wanted was her dad—but of course they hadn't been able to get hold of him. Typical.

Perhaps he should sail home early. It was hard for him to be away. Normally he spent more time in the office running his business than on a boat. This was the longest he'd been away for some time. His stomach curled.

He hung up the phone, receiving a text almost immediately from Ellen with THANK YOU! xx in big capital letters. He loved his sisters more than anything, and right now he felt as if he was being a terrible big brother by taking time off for himself.

'Family emergency sorted,' he said, forcing a jovial tone as he returned to the table.

Chantal sipped her champagne, watching him quietly. 'Everything okay?'

'Fine.'

He looked out to the picture-perfect view of the beach slowly being drowned in darkness. Vulnerability wasn't something he did well—he didn't want her to see that he was anything but his usual cool, calm self. 'Just sex' didn't involve feelings or spilling your guts about family stuff... no more than he had already, anyway. In his defence, that had been to comfort her—not because he'd needed to get it off his chest.

'I should probably head off,' Chantal said, downing the rest of her drink and reaching out to give Kate a friendly hug. 'Thanks for the company.'

'Are you still dancing at the bar?' Scott asked, looking from her to Brodie and back again.

'Yep—I still need to make a living, don't I?' She seemed more comfortable about it than she had previously, there was light at the end of the tunnel. Her contract would run out eventually, and Brodie would make sure she didn't sign on for more work there.

'Don't let the creeps get you down,' Kate said.

'Creeps?' Brodie asked, his protective sensors going off.

'It's nothing.' Chantal shot Kate a look. 'You've seen the place. The clientele isn't exactly the picture of genteel politeness.'

'I'll meet you out the front when you finish,' Brodie said.
Chantal shook her head, shooting him a warning look as if to remind him of their argument last night. 'I'll be fine.'
'I'll meet you out the front.'

CHAPTER TEN

THOUGH SUMMER HAD drawn to a close a few weeks back, the air still hung heavy with humidity. Brodie stood by the railing outside the bar, waiting for Chantal to appear. He'd spent a good five minutes deciding whether or not to go in, but the temptation of hauling her off the stage had been too much to bear, and he didn't want to show her he was having doubts about his feelings towards the temporary nature of their arrangement.

Instead he waited outside, fending off requests for cigarettes, wishing that somehow Chantal had wriggled her way out of the contract. He wasted the time away by texting Ellen, hoping that she didn't hold his absence against him.

'I'm with someone.'

Chantal's voice caught him by surprise. He whipped around and saw her backing away from a big guy whose tank top said 'Team Bogan'. The guy looked at Brodie, sizing him up.

'See.' Chantal gestured to Brodie. 'This is my boyfriend—Axl.'

Brodie raised a brow. *Axl...really?* The guy lumbered away, distracted by a group of girls who didn't appear to have boyfriends waiting for them. Chantal used the opportunity to jog over to him, and sling her arm around his waist.

'Axl was the best you could do?' He shook his head. 'Never picked you for a Guns N' Roses fan.'

'Sorry.' She laughed, holding on to him as they made their way out of the bar's parking lot. 'The band was playing one of their songs as I was walking out. Mum used to listen to them all the time when I was young.'

'Better than the music *I* listened to growing up. Mum was a huge country fan—I hated it.'

Stars winked at them from the inky sky. Away from the hustle and bustle of Sydney the darkness wasn't diluted by the glow from skyscrapers and headlights. It reminded him of home—of the outdoorsy beauty of Queensland he'd grown to love after returning home from Weeping Reef.

'Have you talked to the guy who runs the bar about skipping out early?'

Chantal shook her head. 'No, and I haven't heard back about my audition yet, so I'm not giving up a paying job if there isn't something else to go to.'

'I'll lend you some money.'

'Over my dead body.' She tucked close against him as they walked, melting into him though her tone still revealed a touch of hesitation. 'It's kind of you to offer but I don't take loans—especially when I'm unsure how long it will take me to pay it back.'

'I know you're good for it.'

'Doesn't matter. I'll finish out this contract, see where I am, and figure out my next move.'

'Why are you so against asking for help?' he asked drily.

'I don't need charity.'

They walked through the yacht club and down to where his boat was docked. On board, they sat on the cosy leather-lined seat that curved around the deck. Chantal found a spot next to him, sitting with her head and shoulders resting against his chest. He draped his arm over her and skimmed his fingers along her stomach. It was frighteningly intimate and comfortable. *Familiar.*

'Haven't you heard the saying *Many hands make light work*?'

'Some of those hands get burned,' she said. 'I prefer doing things on my own. That's how it was growing up and I like my independence. Nothing wrong with that.'

'There's a difference between being independent and being stubborn to the point of self-detriment.'

'Asking for help hasn't ever got me anywhere to date. I trust the wrong people.'

'Do you think it's wrong to trust *me*?'

'I trust you as much as I'll ever trust anyone, but I'm still my own person. I do my own thing. That's why this isn't anything but two friends enjoying one another while it lasts.'

'Right.'

Raucous laughter floated on the breeze from a neighbouring boat. Chantal shifted against him, stroking his knuckles with her fingertips. It was a light touch, casual in its intimacy, and yet it flooded him with awareness. She was far from being out of his system. If anything, she'd burrowed herself deep without even trying. Without wanting to.

He couldn't be falling for her—not when he had a life and a family in Queensland to get back to and she had a dream to follow. Different worlds. Disconnected goals. They were wrong, wrong, *wrong*.

'Was everything really okay with your family today?'

A lump lodged in his throat. He didn't want to talk about that now—not when Chantal had made it clear that there was nothing real between them. But then he would be a hypocrite, wouldn't he? He couldn't berate her for not accepting help if she was willing to lend an ear and he didn't take it.

'Nothing major. Lydia was having a bad day. It happens every so often.' He rested his cheek against the top of her head, breathing in the scent of her faded flowery perfume and his coconut shampoo in her hair. 'Ellen was on her own, trying to deal with it. But she's only a kid herself—she needed help.'

'Ellen's the youngest, right?'

'Yeah. She's a good kid—they all are.' He swallowed against the lump in his throat. 'After the accident I was the one who looked after Lydia on a day-to-day basis. She listens to me. Whereas she's big sister to the other girls and yet feels like she can't do anything for them because of her paraplegia.'

'I bet she's grateful she had a big brother to take care of her.'

'She would have preferred to have Dad around. If that didn't make him come home nothing would. But the world didn't stop turning because she couldn't walk any more.' He sighed. 'Mum still had to bring home the bacon...the girls still had to get to school. I was the one who made sure she got to her appointments, made sure she did her exercises, helped her while she was still adjusting to her wheelchair.'

'That must have been tough.' Her hand curled into his and she snuggled farther down against him.

'It's hard to be away from them. Mum's always working, and Dad just...' He shook his head. 'The guy can barely manage a call on their birthdays. He'll disappear for months at a time, then show up out of the blue—usually because he needs money.'

'Where does he disappear to?'

'Who knows? He's a painter, the creative type, and he always seems to be off somewhere unreachable. Then he comes back, tries to make amends with Mum, and it goes well for a while until he asks for money.' Brodie cursed under his breath. 'Every time it happens he breaks the girls' hearts all over again...Mum's included.'

'And your mum's okay with him coming and going?'

'Not really—she did divorce him after all. But she puts her feelings for him before the girls.' Brodie laughed, the sound sharp and hollow. 'See? I told you my family wasn't picture perfect.'

'You don't have to be the parent. You do know that, right?'

But he did have to. Whether he liked it or not, *he* was responsible for looking after those girls. They relied on him—on his advice, on his life experience, on his care. Especially Lydia.

'You shouldn't feel guilty for taking a little time away,' she continued. 'You have to live your own life.'

'I *am* living my own life. I'm here, away from home, seeing my friends and spending time with you.'

'And you feel guilty as all hell, don't you?'

How could she read him like that? Silky hair brushed against his cheek. Her body was warm beneath his hands. How could she read him as though they were far more than friends who happened to be having very casual, very *temporary* sex?

'I have a sense of obligation to my family. What kind of person would I be if I didn't care?'

'I'm not saying you should stop caring. But there are varying levels—it's not all or nothing.' She pushed up, leaning out of his grip. 'Your dad is the one who needs to step up, here—he needs to commit to being a father.'

'Only when hell freezes over.'

'Have you ever talked to him about it?'

'No point.' He shook his head, tightening his grip on her.

In that moment she anchored him. Her questions were digging deep within him. Unlocking the emotion he'd tried to keep buried, allowing him to feel angry about his father.

To see that he'd been suppressing the hurt in order to be a rock for his sisters and his mother.

'Why? Do you think he deserves to shirk his responsibilities and have you pick up the pieces?'

'Of course not. But that doesn't mean I can let the girls go without.'

'No, but maybe you're in a position to try and push your father in the right direction.' She sighed. 'It might allow you to have a little more breathing room…to have the life that you want.'

'I have everything I want.' He gestured to the air. 'Got my boat, got my business. I don't want anything else.'

'Don't you?'

Pink flashed in front of his eyes as her tongue darted out to moisten her lips. She played with the ends of her hair, twirling the strands into a bun and then letting them spiral out around her shoulders.

'Is that all you want out of life?'

Wrapping her arms around herself, she shivered. Tiny ridges of goosebumps patterned her skin.

'Let's go inside. I don't want you getting sick.' He held out a hand and she took it without hesitation. 'Although maybe that would be a good way to get you out of that contract.'

'I'm not getting out of the contract.' She followed him to the kitchen, perching herself on a bar stool. 'I have a sense of obligation too, you know.'

'There's no doubt in my mind about *that*.'

'Why do you say it like that?'

'Your career before everything else. I have no doubt it's the most important thing in your life.'

'It is.' She tilted her head, watching him as he flicked on the coffee machine and pulled two cups from the cupboard. 'What's wrong with that?'

'I think your career is like my family. It's important…
sometimes *too* important.'

'So you agree you need space from your family?' She
grinned, swinging her legs.

'That's about as much agreement as you'll get from me.'

'You're so stubborn!'

'Ha! You should take a look in the mirror some time.'

The coffee machine hissed, steam billowing out of the
nozzle in coils of white condensation. Black liquid ran
into the cups, filling the air with a rich, roasted scent. He
splashed milk into the first cup and handed it to Chantal.
A grin spread over her lips and she blew on the steam,
waiting for him to make the first move.

She wore the black skirt and white top she'd had on at
drinks earlier that evening, but she'd ditched her shoes
and jewellery. The gold threads in her top glinted under
the light, making it seem as if she were glowing. It wasn't
possible for her to look any more at home on the boat. He
wondered what it would be like if they both tossed their
obligations overboard and set sail. They had a boat—he
had money. It could be the two of them. Together. Alone.

*What is it about 'just sex' that you don't understand?
She doesn't want you like that. You're just a body. A good
lay.*

'Are we going to keep dancing around like this or are
you going to invite me to bed?'

She looked over the edge of her cup, the white porcelain
barely hiding a cheeky smile. Her dark lashes fluttered and
warm pink heat spread through her cheeks.

'Who's insatiable now?'

'Time's ticking. I want to enjoy this arrangement while
I still can.'

It doesn't have to stop.

The words teetered on the edge of his tongue, willing
his lips to open so they could pour out. But he couldn't

let them. Instead he walked around to the other side of the breakfast bar and pulled her into his arms. His lips crushed down on hers, seeking out the hot, open delight of her mouth. The taste of fresh coffee mingled with the honeyed sweetness of her.

'As you wish.'

Chantal woke to the sound of something vibrating, but the haze of slumber refused to release her. Groggy, she pushed herself into a sitting position, smiling as Brodie reached for her in his sleep. Fingertips brushed her thigh and he sighed, rolling over. Blond lashes threw feathered shadows across his cheekbones and his full lips melted into a gentle smile.

'You look so damn innocent,' she muttered, brushing a lock of hair from his forehead. He didn't stir. 'But I know better.'

The vibrating stopped and a loud ping signalled a text message. Removing Brodie's hand from her leg, she set off in search of her phone. It wasn't in the bedroom, though everything else of hers appeared to be—a lacy thong, matching bra, white and gold top, stretchy black skirt.

A laugh bubbled in her throat. Her clothes were strewn so far around the room it looked almost staged. But her aching limbs told the truth. They'd spent another amazing, pulse-racing, heart-fluttering, boundary-breaking night together.

Danger! Emotions approaching—full speed ahead.

It was just sex…wasn't it? She could stop any time. *Spoken like a true addict, Turner.*

Huffing, she stomped out to the kitchen. She didn't want to be having thoughts like this. Brodie was a bit of fun. A friend, yes, but nothing more. She couldn't let it be any more…not when he'd already shown that he had the same protective urges as her ex. No matter how well intentioned he was, she would *not* let herself be smothered again.

A flashing blue light caught her attention. One new voicemail. It had better not be the bar, pushing her to extend her contract. She'd officially be admitting defeat if she signed with them for another month. Then again, it wasn't as if she had other offers to consider, and this thing with Brodie had to come to an end. He'd be sailing home at some point, and she couldn't exactly stow away on his boat to avoid her problems. No, she needed an apartment, a job...a *better* job. She needed her independence back.

She tapped in her password and dialled the voicemail number. Her pulse shot up as the caller introduced himself as being from the Harbour Dance Company. They wanted her to come in for a chat about the company and a second audition. She hadn't flunked it!

By the time she hung up the phone Brodie had ambled into the kitchen. Cotton pyjama pants hung low on his hips. A trail of blond hair dipped below the waistband. He was a god—a tattooed, tanned, six-pack-adorned god.

'Good news?'

'How could you tell?' She put her phone back on the table and bounded over to him, throwing her arms around his neck.

'Your greetings are usually a little less enthusiastic than this,' he said, chuckling, and lifted her up so that her legs instinctively wrapped around his waist. 'Not to mention you were bouncing around so much I thought you'd been stung by a jellyfish.'

'They want a second audition!' She didn't have time to counter his teasing. She was so brimming with relief that she had to let it out.

'Why wouldn't they? You're pretty damn fantastic.' He backed her up against the breakfast bar, bringing his mouth down to hers. 'So that means we'll be heading back to Sydney?'

'*I'll* be heading back to Sydney. The audition isn't till the end of the week, and you're taking off then…aren't you?'

He hesitated, the jovial grin slipping from his lips as he avoided her eyes. 'Yeah, I'll be heading back soon.'

Had he been thinking about staying? For *her*? That was too confusing a thought to process, so she pushed a hand through his hair and kissed the tip of his nose.

'No more swanning around on yachts for me.'

'No.'

'All good things must come to an end, as they say.' She wished the cheerful tone of her voice mirrored her thoughts. But the words had as much substance as fairy floss.

What was wrong with her? This was *Brodie*. Beach bum. Playboy. Dreamer. Drifter. Flake.

Only he wasn't any of those things in reality. He was a successful businessman. A friend, a great cook, a family man, the best sex of her life. He was complex, layered, and not at all as she'd labelled him. Could it get any worse?

'We should celebrate,' he said, cutting through her thoughts by setting her down. 'How about I take you out on the water and we'll have lunch?'

'I have to be back for a shift tonight, but that would be great.'

'Of course,' he said, a hint of bitterness tainting his voice. 'How could I forget about the bar?'

'Don't start, Brodie…it won't go on forever.' She wasn't going to let that scummy bar ruin their celebration.

'Why don't you have a shower and I'll get us underway.'

'Are you trying to tell me I smell again?' She shoved him in the shoulder and his smile returned…almost.

'You smell like sex.'

'Gee, I wonder why.' She rolled her eyes and skipped off towards his room.

Some time later she emerged, having spent longer than usual showering. Water helped her to think. She often did her best problem-solving under the steady stream of a showerhead. Unfortunately today seemed to be an exception to the rule. No solution to her confusion about Brodie had materialised. She was *still* stuck between wanting to enjoy their time for what it was and the niggling feeling that perhaps it was more than she wanted to admit.

Dangerous thoughts... Remember what happened last time you gave in. Remember the smothering you didn't see coming until it was too late.

She wandered to the upper area of the boat, spotting Brodie standing at the wheel and looking as though he'd been born to do exactly that. Wind whipped through his hair, tossing the blond strands around his face as the boat moved. Blond stubble had thickened along his chiselled jaw, roughening his usually charming face into something sexier and more masculine.

'Clean as a whistle,' she announced, stepping down into the driving area of the boat. 'Can I join you at the wheel, Captain?'

'You may.'

'Wow, there are a lot of dials.' Chantal hadn't yet been up to this area of the boat. It looked like the cockpit of a plane.

'It's a fairly sophisticated piece of machinery. A slight step up from your average tugboat.' He winked.

'It feels like you're free up here, doesn't it?'

The sparkling blue of the ocean stretched for miles around, and the sun glinted off the waves like a scattering of tiny diamonds.

'That's what I love most about it. I can think out here.'

A shadow crossed over his face. 'It's like I have no prob-lems at all.'

'Do you ever wonder what would happen if you sailed away and never came back?'

'Are you trying to tell me something?' His smile didn't ring true, the crinkle not quite reaching his eyes.

'I'm serious. Don't you think it would be great to go somewhere new? Start over?' That sounded like the most appealing idea she'd ever come up with. A fresh start. No baggage. A clean slate unmarked by her previous mistakes.

He shrugged. 'Yeah, I think about it for five seconds and then I realise what a stupid idea it is.'

'Why?'

'I couldn't leave my family.'

'Even if it was the thing you wanted to do most in the world?'

'It would take something pretty spectacular to make me seriously consider it. To date, nothing has come close.'

Chantal bit down on her lip, hating herself for allow-ing his words to sting. He was clearly drawing a line in the sand, defining their relationship...or lack thereof. She should be happy. He'd absolved her of any guilt about leav-ing him at the end of the week. But the words cut into her as real and painful as any blade.

'Doesn't hurt to fantasise,' she said wistfully.

'Sometimes it does.' He looked as though he were about to continue but his face changed suddenly. 'We're going to stop soon, but you might want to head portside in a minute.'

Chantal looked from left to right. 'Portside?'

'Sorry—boat-speak.' Brodie pointed to a section of the railing to his left. 'Stand over there.'

'You're not going to tip me overboard, are you?'

He smirked. 'Don't tempt me.'

Chantal went to the railing, holding on to the metal bar with both hands. 'What am I looking for?'

'You'll know it when you see it.'

Beautiful as the view was, she couldn't see anything much. They were clearly approaching land, but the fuzzy green mounds still looked a while away. She shielded her eyes with her hand, searching.

Something glimmered below the water—a shadow. Holy crap, was that a *shark*? Moments later the water broke, and a group of a dozen dolphins raced alongside the boat in a blur of grey and splashing blue.

'Did you see that?' Chantal shouted, leaning over the railing to watch the majestic creatures leap out of the water over and over.

They were so sleek. So fast and playful.

'Careful!' Brodie called out with a smile on his face. 'Don't fall in.'

'There's so many of them.'

She watched, mesmerised by the fluid way the dolphins moved—as if they were trying to keep up with the boat. Their smooth bodies sliced through the water, their beaked faces appearing to smile. They looked joyful. Uninhibited.

Chantal could feel the heat of Brodie's gaze on her, boring holes through the thin layer of her ankle-length dress. Right now his boat was the most amazing place in the world. How would she ever leave it at the end of the week?

CHAPTER ELEVEN

SEEING CHANTAL'S FACE when she discovered the dolphins had melted his insides. The sparkle in her eye, her squeak of delight, the way she'd hung over the railing as though she was desperate to jump into the water with them…it had been too much.

After the dolphins had moved on he'd steered them to Nelson Bay and moored in the spot normally reserved for one of the dolphin and whale-watching companies. After ordering Chantal off to the shower that morning he'd called in a favour with a friend who ran the mooring services for the Port Stephens region. Now they had a couple of hours for lunch before he'd need to leave the area and head back to Newcastle.

A spread of smoked salmon, bagels with cream cheese and fresh fruit covered the table that sat in front of the curved leather and wood seat. He'd also popped a bottle of champagne, which sat in a silver ice bucket.

'Did you know the dolphins were going to be there?' Chantal asked, taking a hearty bite out of a bagel. Cream cheese spilled forward, coating her upper lip, and her pink tongue darted out to capture it.

He remembered her obsession with bagels back from when they were at Weeping Reef together. Despite being slim as a rail, she'd devoured the doughy delights every morning for breakfast. Always with cream cheese. God, he had to stop looking at her mouth. She dived in for another bite, her eyes fluttering shut as she savoured the flavour.

'You never know for sure. But there is a group of dolphins who live in the area, so it's common to see them.' He took a swig of his water.

'They live here?'

'Not specifically in Nelson Bay, but in the general Port Stephens area. It's a big pod too—about eighty dolphins, I think.'

'Wow.' She sighed. 'They're so beautiful. I've always wanted to do one of those swim-with-the-dolphins things.'

'They're a lot of fun. The bottlenecks especially—they're very playful.'

Her eyes widened. 'You've done it? I'm so jealous.'

'Yeah.' Brodie nodded, a memory flickering. 'We did it as kids once...me and Lydia. Before her accident.'

For a moment he wondered if she would dig further, ask about Lydia's accident. Instead she said, 'What do they feel like?'

'They're smooth—kind of rubbery.'

'What do they eat?'

He laughed, taken by her intense curiosity. 'Fish, squid...that kind of thing.'

Lying back on her chair, she kicked her legs out and crossed her ankles. A contented sigh escaped her lips. 'I'm so full. That salmon was amazing.'

'You're welcome.'

She turned her head, shielding her eyes with her hand. 'This is the best celebration I could have asked for... although it's not a done deal. I might flunk the next audition.'

'Always thinking positive—that's what I like about you,' he teased.

'Nothing wrong with being realistic.' She sighed. 'I'm

trying to protect myself, I guess. I don't want to be disappointed if I don't get it.'

'If they want a second audition then they obviously saw something they liked.'

'That's true.' She twirled a strand of hair around one finger.

'You're immensely talented—you know that, right?' He chewed on his own bagel, concentrating on the food so that he could hide the conflicting emotions doing battle within him.

'Let's just hope the Harbour Dance Company agree with you.' She paused. 'I've had fun staying on the boat.'

He'd hoped to hear *with you* emerge from her lips, but she stopped short. *Stop waiting to hear that she's fallen for you. She hasn't.*

'I've had *fun* too.'

He half-heartedly waggled his brows and she swatted at him, laughing.

'I don't just mean the sex, Brodie. I mean I've had fun… hanging out.'

'Hanging out? What are we? Teenagers?' he teased.

She shook her head. 'Way to make a girl feel awkward. Can't a friend give another friend a compliment?'

Friend. There it was again—the invisible barrier between them. He'd broken his rule by sleeping with her in the first place. Funny thing was, that rule had always been in place to preserve the friendship, so that when he rejected any serious advances the other person wouldn't get hurt. He'd never counted on it going the other way—not when he had his priorities sorted out and they certainly didn't include a serious relationship.

'I prefer my compliments to be of the physical variety.'

'You're not nearly as sleazy as you try to be,' she said.

'I'm not *trying* to be anything.' It came out way too defensive. Why didn't he just hold up a flag that said *Emotional sore point. Proceed with caution.*

'Yes, you are. You're hell-bent on being the casual, laid-back, cool-as-a-cucumber fun-time guy.'

'You seemed to believe I *was* that guy.'

'I didn't know you then.' Her olive eyes glowed in the bright afternoon light, the golden edges of her hair glinting like precious metal. 'But I do now.'

'You know what I want you to know.'

'No way.' Her lips pursed. 'You sailed a yacht out here to show me dolphins...you packed a champagne lunch for me. All because I got a second audition—not even a proper job. That's not a fun-time guy.'

'What is it, then?'

He was giving her a chance to be honest, to open up to him. But the shutters went down over her eyes and colour seeped into her cheeks. Her hands folded into a neat parcel in her lap. Shutdown mode enabled.

'You're a good person, Brodie. I wish we'd got to be real friends sooner.'

There was that F-word again. If he heard it come out of her mouth one more time he was going to throw something. Clearly he was going out of his mind. Girls didn't rattle him—that wasn't how he acted. On the scale of annoyance, girl problems ranked somewhere between lining up at the supermarket and typos. In other words it fell into the bundle of crap he didn't care about.

'We should probably head back.' He pushed up from his chair, feeling the burn of the afternoon sun on his legs. 'Don't want to make you late for work.'

'Yeah, that thorn in my side.' She sighed.

She followed him around as he prepared the boat to return to Newcastle. Her anxious energy irritated him—partially because he felt she had no reason to be anxious, and partially because it made him want to bundle her up and kiss her until she relaxed. The woman had an emotional stronghold over him that was both dangerous and stupid. He already had four women to take care of—five if he counted his mother. He didn't need a sixth.

'You don't need to pick me up from the bar tonight,' she said once they were back at the helm, with the boat cruising out of the marina.

'I'll be there.' No way he'd let her walk back to the boat on her own.

'I can stay at the accommodation, if you like.'

'You're welcome to stay on the boat until I have to sail back. That hasn't changed.'

He didn't look at her, but her nervousness permeated the air. She knew he was angry with her. He had to keep his emotions in check.

'I want you to stay.'

'Okay.' She put her hand over his. 'Thanks.'

Don't grab her hand...don't grab her hand. 'No worries.'

'I'll be happy when I finish up at the bar. It's certainly been a learning experience.' She let out a small laugh. 'Although the crowd is a bit rough for my liking.'

'A *bit*?' He stole a glance at her and regretted it immediately. Make-up-free, hair flowing, she looked young and vulnerable. *You're weak, Mitchell, absolutely weak.*

'Okay, a lot. It wouldn't be so bad if the guys weren't so handsy.'

'What do you mean, *handsy*?'

'You know—some guys seem to think by buying a few drinks they can have free handling of the dancers.' She rolled her eyes. 'Pigs.'

White-hot rage brewed in his stomach. 'Dammit, Chantal. Why didn't you tell me?'

'Because it's not your problem—it's *mine*.' She spoke

calmly, but she crossed her arms and stepped backwards. 'Besides, last time you came into the bar you flipped out.'

'Of course I did!' He fought to wrangle the frustration and anger warring inside him. 'It's like you refuse to look after yourself just to prove a point.'

'I'm not trying to prove a point.' She gritted her teeth. 'Anyway, I had a word with them and told them to back off.'

'Jeez, you had *a word* with them? I'm sure that will make *all* the difference.' He shook his head, gritting his teeth at the thought of these grubby morons touching her. 'You need to tell me these things.'

'I don't *need* to tell you anything.' Her eyes flashed like two green flames. Her lips were pressed into a flat line and her breath came in short, irritated stutters. 'It's not your job to protect me.'

'What if they attacked you? What if you stayed at the accommodation and they followed you?' Nausea rocked his stomach. If anything ever happened to her...

'You're not my knight in shining armour, Brodie.' She spoke through gritted teeth, her hands balled by her sides. 'I can look after myself. Don't you get that?'

'All I see is someone who's too damn stubborn to ask for help.'

She folded her arms across her chest. The air pulsed around her as she narrowed her eyes at him. 'Independence is important to me.'

'At the cost of intelligence, it seems.'

'Oh, that's rich coming from you.'

'What the hell is *that* supposed to mean?' His blood boiled. He couldn't remember the last time he'd felt this... this *everything*. Emotions collided inside him, strong and flying at full speed.

'You won't live your life because you think it's your job to take care of every tiny thing for your family. You live

in guilt because your father left but you won't even confront him about it. You're scared.'

'I'm not scared.'

'Yes, you *are*.' She jabbed a finger at him.

With her composure out of the window, Chantal let frustration and anger flow out of her unchecked.

'You won't let yourself feel anything for anyone outside your family.'

'Oh, and that's as bad as dancing at some skanky bar
where you're not safe?' He shook his head. 'Yeah—real
smart.'

'Dancing at that bar might seem stupid to you, but I
need to make it on my own. I will *not* let someone else
tell me what to do.' *Least of all someone who's supposed
to be a 'no-strings tension-reliever'.*

'Who would try, Chantal? It's clear you won't listen to
anyone else. You're so goddamn bull-headed.'

'Try looking in a mirror some time.'

In a rush, tears welled up with the force of a tidal wave.
She had to get out. *Now!*

She flew down the stairs to the lower deck and didn't
stop until she reached the kitchen. Her chest heaved, and
she was dragging in each breath as though it resisted her
with the force of an army. Cheeks burning, she felt the
toxic warmth seeping down her neck and closing around
her windpipe. She would *not* have a meltdown in front of
him...not again.

The smooth marble bench was cool against her palms.
Was he coming after her? *And who would sail the boat
then? Idiot. Of course he's not coming after you.*

Twisting the kitchen tap with a shaking hand, she bent
down to splash some water onto her face before filling a
glass. Brodie's yacht had made her feel free when they'd
sailed out of Newcastle that morning, but now...now it
was as if the walls were closing in, crushing her, trapping

her. She sipped, savouring the sensation of the cold liquid slipping down the back of her throat.

It was time to end things with Brodie. Chantal only ever got mad when she cared—she only ever lost her temper when something important was on the line. Even when Scott had left Weeping Reef she hadn't been angry…just guilty because it had all ended so suddenly and because of her inability to control herself. But she'd known deep down that Scott wasn't the man for her.

What did that say about Brodie and the way she was feeling now?

It's nothing. You had a great time with him, he provided you a nice place to stay, but now it's back to reality. No more messing around. You've got an audition to nail and a job to finish.

When they arrived back at Newcastle, Brodie didn't materialise on the lower deck. Chantal decided to avoid him by getting ready for her shift. Smoky shadow made her eyes look wide and alluring…a clear gloss played up her natural pout. The make-up gave her something to hide behind—another persona to help her get through the shift. The patrons of the bar saw only the image she wanted them to see, not the real her.

But Brodie had seen the real her. The scared girl with too-high expectations, a faltering career and a predisposition for panic attacks. Appealing stuff.

She bit down on her lip so hard the metallic tang of blood seeped onto her tongue. She couldn't afford to lose it now. A second audition with the Harbour Dance Company was a sign that she was heading in the right direction. A sign that perhaps everything would turn out the way she wanted it to. Or did she want more than that?

Her packed bags sat by the kitchen bench. How long had she been living out of a bag now? Too long. The rest of her belongings had been stashed at her mother's place, with a few extra essentials in the back of her car…if it was still in the bar's car park after all this time.

Oddly, she didn't care. Numbness had taken over the anger, smoothing down the edges of her emotions until she felt smooth and cold. Closed off…the way she preferred it.

Hoisting her bag over her shoulder, she slipped her feet into a pair of ballet flats and made her way onto the deck. Brodie's voice floated down from the upper level. He was talking to one of his sisters. A smile tugged at the corner of her lips. He had a certain tone for his sisters. Tough, and yet so full of love it made her heart ache. No one spoke to *her* like that—not even her mother.

Should she bid him a formal goodbye? Thank him for giving her a place to stay? Probably.

Instead she left, heading towards the bar with a hard knot rocking the pit of her stomach. *Keep going…one foot in front of the other. You need distance and so does he.*

She was doing the right thing. Staying would only be prolonging the inevitable breakdown of their relationship… whatever *that* was. She didn't know how to label it.

At some point he'd been a mere acquaintance, a secret crush. Then a friend. Then a friend with benefits… And now?

She squeezed her eyes shut, willing away the persistent thumping at the base of her skull. Dancing tonight would be tough, but she had to get through it. Light was most certainly at the end of the tunnel…so long as she kept Brodie out of her head.

'What's wrong, Brodes? You sound upset.' Lydia's voice floated through the phone, her concern twisting something sharp in his chest.

'I'm fine. It's the sound of relaxation. You know how long it's been since I took a holiday.'

'Yeah.' She laughed. 'You work too hard. You don't sound relaxed, though.'

'It's nothing.'

'Swear?'

He gritted his teeth. He'd never sworn on a lie to any one of his sisters and he wasn't about to start now. Perhaps if he didn't say anything she'd get bored and move on.

Lydia audibly smirked into the silence. 'What's her name?'

Damn. 'Her name doesn't matter.'

'Oh, come on. I don't get to do the boy thing much—how about a little vicarious living?'

She said it with such calm acceptance that he wanted to hang up the phone and get to her in any way possible. It wasn't fair that she didn't have a boyfriend simply because she couldn't walk. Although with the way Chantal had left him with a permanent imbalance perhaps it was a good thing.

'Her name is Chantal. She's a friend.'

'But you want more?'

'No, I don't. We agreed to keep things…friendly.' His brow creased. He was so *not* talking about this with his little sister.

'Do you love her?'

He hesitated. 'Of course not. I only have enough love for you guys… There's only so many women a guy can have in his life before he goes crazy.'

Lydia huffed and he could practically see her rolling her green eyes at him. 'You sound like Dad.'

There was a scary image. *I take care of you girls. I don't run away from my family when the whim takes me.*

'When was the last time you heard from Dad?'

'Touché,' Lydia said with a sigh. 'Why won't you be more than friends with Chantal?'

'We're not having this conversation, Lyds.'

'But—'

'Not. Having. This. Conversation.'

'OMG, you're *so* boring.'

He could hear the laughter in her voice and he thanked the heavens that she was having a better day today.

'I miss you.'

'I miss you too.' There was a slight pause on the other end of the line. 'I *would* like it if you got married one day.'

'Marriage isn't for me.' He shook his head, wondering how on earth he'd got roped into talking about relationships. 'Besides, you already have three sisters. You don't need another one.'

'But I might not get married and I'd like to be in a wedding. Why wouldn't you want to do it?'

Brodie swallowed the lump in his throat at the thought of all the things he took for granted. Why wouldn't he want to do it? Did he even *know* why? He told himself he didn't have room in his life for a relationship…but then again Chantal was different from his ex. She wasn't clingy or needy…quite the opposite! He'd sworn off long-term relationships because he knew he'd have to choose between them and his family. What if he'd been wrong? What if he *could* have both?

'You'll get married one day, Lyds. Not until I've checked the guy out, though. I'll need to make sure he's good enough for you.'

She laughed. 'You'd better not scare any potential husbands away.'

'Watch me.'

He hung up the phone and made a mental note to pop in and see Lydia as soon as he got back to Queensland. Perhaps he'd head back earlier than planned. It wasn't as if Chantal would be coming back to the boat after their argument. Without her he didn't have a reason to stay.

And where would *she* stay? A cold tremor ran the length

of his spine, settling in the pit of his stomach. The bar ac-commodation wasn't safe, he believed that even more now after what she'd told him today. He'd noted the single lock on the door while Chantal had packed her bags in front of him. That door needed at least another five locks be-fore it became remotely secure. Not that the cheap wood door would withstand a well-aimed kick or the swing of a crowbar...

He dropped onto a sun lounger and put his head in his hands. How had it gone downhill so quickly? One minute they were out on the ocean, racing the dolphins, and the next they were yelling at one another. That was definitely not in the vein of their friends-with-benefits arrangement.

Maybe he could convince her to let him pay for a hotel room. There was a suitable beach resort down the road from the bar. It wasn't anything fancy, but it would be more secure than her room. He could give her a couple hundred bucks, make sure she was safe, and then leave her the hell alone.

Would she take the money from him? Not likely, but he had to try. The thought of anything happening to her filled him with cold, hard dread. He cared about her. She was a friend—of *course* he cared about her. That was nor-mal, wasn't it?

He paced the length of the helm, his muscles tightening with each agitated step. Chantal valued her independence, that was for sure, but he had a right to step in if she was endangering herself. It was his duty...as a friend.

Jogging down the stairs to the lower deck, he went on the hunt for his wallet and phone. She was gone. Her bags were nowhere to be found and the bedroom was so tidy it was as if she'd never been there. But her presence hung in the air like perfume—sweet and memory-triggering. All the scraps of lace that had littered the floor after their various escapades had been removed, and the small pile of her jewellery on his bedside table had vanished too.

He snatched up his keys from the hook on his bedroom wall and jammed his wallet into the pocket of his shorts. She was going to be royally pissed at him trying to buy her a room, but he didn't care. Having her angry at him was better than any of the other alternatives. She'd have to deal with her anger. He wasn't going to take no for an answer.

CHAPTER TWELVE

BACKSTAGE AT THE BAR, Chantal tried to psych herself up for her performance. Truth was she wanted to run away with her tail between her legs and never come back. But she was a professional, a trooper. She never backed down.

Part of her wanted to get out there on that stage to prove a point. Brodie had treated her as if she was made of crystal—as if she'd break with the slightest knock. But she didn't break. She'd been through her share of tough times and she *always* kept going. No matter what.

'Don't look so down, honey.' A blonde girl in a sparkling corset pouted at her. 'If I had natural boobs like that *I* wouldn't be frowning.'

Chantal instinctively crossed her arms over her chest. 'I'm fine.'

'Is this your first time dancing?'

'No, not at all.' Did she look *that* nervous? Hell, what had Brodie done to her? She was wound up tighter than a spring.

'It'll be okay.' The blonde nodded and gave her shoulder a light pat. The woman's long silver nails glinted like tiny blades. 'Don't let the audience frighten you. They're big old lugs. Only here for the tits and the booze, never mind that fabulous dancing we all do.'

Chantal couldn't help but smile. The blonde gave a little shimmy, flicking the black fringe edging her corset back and forth. Her stockings stopped at mid-thigh, biting into her generous flesh, and she wore black gloves that stretched up over her elbows. She looked at ease with herself...with what she was doing.

'Just have fun. Leave your worries behind!' She sang the last few words, twirling and shaking her ample booty.

'I think I need to take a leaf out of your book,' Chantal said, smiling.

'Good idea. I always get a little tipsy before I dance.' The blonde leaned in conspiratorially. 'A couple of shots of tequila. *Boom!* Loose hips.'

Chantal practised her routine in the small space next to the mirror-lined bench. Sure, this wasn't the best place on earth, and it wasn't what she wanted for her career, but she could get through it. To hell with Brodie. She'd be fine and she didn't need anyone else to take care of her. She *would* stand on her own two feet.

The dancer before her gyrated on stage, using the pole to complete some gravity-defying tricks. The audience roared, catcalls and wolf-whistles drowning out all but the heavy thump of the bass. Then it was her turn. She peeked out as the other dancer finished up. The crowd had swelled considerably since she'd first arrived.

Then she spotted Brodie. He was unmistakable. Sitting in the front row, arms folded across his chest, biceps on display...most likely on purpose. The blood drained from her face and her confidence followed it until the world tilted beneath her feet.

What the hell was he doing here?

Her music started but her feet were rooted to the ground. Someone shoved her in the back and she stumbled a little as she walked on stage. The audience didn't seem to notice. They cheered and hooted as she swung her hips, pivoting on one foot with a dainty flick of her hair. Under Brodie's intense stare she might as well have been naked. His eyes seemed to penetrate her, seeing all that she wanted to conceal.

He didn't smile, and his eyes certainly didn't sparkle the way they normally did. Had *she* turned him into this hardened lump? Where was the free and easy Brodie she'd fallen for?

And had she really fallen for him…even after everything that had happened today?

Confusion made her head fuzzy, the thoughts clashing in her mind. It was nothing—just a fling. She shook her head, trying to dislodge the warring emotions.

The steps of her choreography eluded her, but she had to keep going. Close to the edge of the stage she felt a hand brush by her—not Brodie's. A portly man with a heavy beard and mean eyes leered up at her. Her skin crawled and she backed away, still clinging to her stage presence though she was sure she'd never danced so terribly in all her life.

Brodie had leant over to the man, his face red and indecipherable words falling from his lips. For a moment she would have sworn a fight would break out, but it didn't. The bass thumped at odd intervals with the pounding in her head…everything unravelled. Fast.

She rushed off stage before her time was up, ducking her head at the curious stares of the other dancers and ignoring the cutting remarks from the manager as she scuffed her feet into her sneakers and grabbed her keys.

Outside the change room people swarmed the crowded space of the bar, the smell of beer and body odour making the air heavy and thick. Swallowing against the nausea, she pushed through, swatting away invasive hands and avoiding lingering stares. If she didn't get outside… Well, it wouldn't be pretty.

Brodie had got up from his chair. Chantal spotted him in her peripheral vision but didn't stop. This was all his fault! He shouldn't have come here thinking he could distract her, making her look like an idiot in front of all these people. As much as she didn't care about their opinions, she was still dancing. Forgetting her choreography was *unforgivable.*

'Chantal!'

How could she have let herself fall for him? The way he'd acted tonight *proved* he was the wrong guy for her. He was just like her ex: over-protective...ready to smother her.

She headed towards the stairs, running down them as fast as she could while dodging two people kissing up against the wall. Downstairs a heavy metal band thrashed about on stage, the drummer's double kicks resonating through her, the beat reverberating right down to her bones.

She stumbled outside, tripping over a pair of feet in her desperation for escape. The cool air rushed into her mouth, was trapped where her throat was closing in. She gasped, sucking the air in greedily and forcing each breath down like a pill without water. How could she have forgotten her choreography? *How?* She balled her shaking hands, wishing she could crawl into a crack in the ground and disappear forever.

'Chantal!' Brodie's voice rang out in the car park, muted by the music from inside the bar. 'Wait—'

The deep rumble of a motorcycle raced past and drowned out the rest of his words. For a moment she kept walking, each purposeful step slamming into the ground. What would happen if she kept going? Tempting as it was, she couldn't quit—she couldn't. Not when things were turning around.

'I'm trying to protect you.' His voice carried on the night air.

Chantal whirled around, her body tense, like a snake about to strike. She locked her arms down by her sides. 'You distracted me up there. I forgot my steps because I couldn't concentrate on anything but whether or not you were going to start a fight.'

'I'm here to make sure you're safe—not to distract you.' His brows pulled down, a crease forming in his forehead. 'I only wanted to make sure you had somewhere safe to stay.'

'I'm not coming back to the boat.'

He shook his head. 'I was planning to pay for a hotel room for you. I'm thinking about your best interests.'

For some reason his words cut right through her chest, making her head pound and her stomach turn. Safety...protection...best interests. These were all words she'd heard before—the vocabulary of a control freak.

'Why don't you trust me, Chantal?'

'You told me I didn't *have* to trust you.' Her voice wobbled and she cringed. 'That was part of the deal.'

His eyes flashed; his mouth pulled into a grim line. 'I thought you'd change your mind.'

'I haven't.'

He raked a hand through his hair, the blond strands falling straight back into place over his eyes. He'd come straight from the boat, still wearing his shorts and boat shoes from their trip to Nelson Bay. The black ink of his anchor tattoo peeked out from the rolled-up sleeve of a crisp blue shirt. Damn him for looking so utterly delectable when she wanted nothing more than to throw her shoe at his head.

What had happened to the laid-back Brodie she knew? Did all guys turn into 'me Tarzan, you Jane' types as soon as you slept with them?

'Have you changed your mind about *anything*?' He stepped forward, folding his arms across his chest.

'Like whether or not I should finish my contract here?' She shrugged, hoping she looked as though she cared a lot less than she did. 'I'm a professional dancer. I can't quit.'

'That wasn't what I was talking about.'

'What *are* you talking about, then, Brodie? Because I sure as hell have no idea.'

His jaw twitched, and the muscles in his neck corded as he drew a long breath. 'What about your desire to do everything on your own?'

'That's how I *need* to do it.'

At least that was what she'd believed most of her life. But somehow she didn't feel so convinced any more. *Remember what happened when you got married... You trusted him and look how that turned out. Mum did it all on her own—you can too.*

'Why?' He took the last few steps towards her until there was no space between them and his hands gripped her shoulders. '*Why* do you think you need to do everything on your own?'

'Because it's safer that way.' She shut her eyes, wishing her brain would stop registering the scent of him and firing up all the parts she needed to stay quiet at the moment. 'I'm sick of being a charity case. I want to do something on my own that I can be proud of. I *need* it.'

'You can be independent without pushing away everyone who feels something for you.'

Blood rushed in her ears. The roaring made it hard to think straight. 'Are you trying to tell me *you* feel something for me?'

That was exactly what he was saying, wasn't it? He *did* have feelings for her. Why would he keep chasing her if he didn't?

'What if I do?'

'That would go against our agreement.' Her olive-green eyes were wide, like two shimmering moons, begging him not to continue.

If he admitted to caring about her and she rejected him what would happen next? He'd never see her again. The thought of a life without her seemed pointless. Colour-less. Dull.

'We're supposed to be friends,' she whispered.

'We are.'

'That's all I have room for. I don't want a relationship right now. I want to get my career sorted. I've worked my whole life for this. I'm not stopping now.'

'You do know you can have more than one thing in life, don't you?' He couldn't help the words coming out with a derisive tone. How could she be so narrow-minded?

Hypocrite.

'Can you? I thought family was *your* one thing.'

She stepped backwards and he let her slip out of his grip.

'Someone told me I was too scared to invest in anyone outside my family. Maybe that person was right.'

'No. Family should come first for you.' Chantal shook her head. 'Go back to Queensland, Brodie. Go home.'

'Who's scared now?' He hated himself for the waver in his voice. She'd managed to do what no other woman ever had—she'd made him feel something. She'd made him want to stay.

'*I* am, Brodie. I'm scared.' She looked at him with a blank face. 'I'm scared for my career, so that's what I'm focusing on right now. Please don't follow me.'

With that she turned and left him standing in the middle of the parking lot. Her silhouette faded into the night and every nerve ending in his body fired, telling him to go after her. But she'd made it clear her life had no room for a relationship. No room for him.

If she wasn't going to let him in there was no point hanging around. He was stupid to have even tried. Of course she wanted nothing more from him. How had he fallen into that trap? *He* was supposed to walk away—it was what he always did.

'You're a goddamn idiot,' he muttered, unsure if he were talking to himself or to her.

By Friday, Brodie was ready to sail home. His travel bag was packed, but he hadn't been able to convince himself to go. Instead he'd headed back to Sydney, in the hope that a change of scenery could pull him out of his incredible funk.

The view from the boat should have cured any bad feelings he had, and the sunlight sparkling off the water and the girls in their tiny shorts and tank tops was his definition of nirvana. Not today, though.

Humid air clung to his sweat-drenched body. He'd hoped going for a run would allow him to burn off the agitated energy that had kept him awake the last few nights. It hadn't. Since then he'd called the office, video chatted with the family, and run until his legs trembled. *Now what?*

The shower beckoned. He stripped, hoping the rush of cool water against his sizzling skin might ease the confusing thoughts in his head. But the normally soothing sound of water against tiles gave him space to think…something he needed like a hole in the head.

He was officially broken.

A noise caught his attention. The vibration of his phone against the benchtop, sounding like insects buzzing. Who would be calling him? The guy who managed his office had already told him to butt out until his holiday was officially up. Apparently things were running like clockwork, and he'd told Brodie he sounded as if he hadn't had any rest at all.

Brodie rubbed his eyes and tilted his face up to the spray. Exhaustion weighed down his limbs. No wonder… He was pretty sure he'd seen each hour tick over on his clock last night.

What if Chantal was calling?

He wrenched at the taps, shutting off the water, and stepped out of the shower. He grabbed a towel and wrapped it around his waist, checking the ID flashing up on his phone. Of course it wasn't her. She'd made it damn clear there was nothing between them. That didn't stop the way his body sprang to action at the thought of her contacting him.

Pathetic.

'Hello?'

'Hey, man.' Scott's voice boomed over the line. 'Want to grab a drink?'

The last thing he wanted was to see Scott face to face. His friend would know in an instant that things had gone south. 'I'm actually having a little time out at the moment.'

'You're back in Queensland?'

'No, not yet.' He'd been so rattled by the encounter with Chantal that he'd hightailed it back up the coast to Sydney without telling *anyone*. Not even Scott.

'Everything okay?'

'Nothing major,' he lied, padding to his bedroom.

'Work problems?'

He paused, unsure how much he wanted to reveal. But Scott's pushing meant he knew something was up. 'Not exactly.'

A chuckle came down the line. 'Let me guess—it starts with C and ends with L.'

'Spelling was never my strong suit.' He tried to make light of Scott's words but it sounded hollow, even to him.

'What happened?'

'I don't know. One minute it was fine—*we* were fine—and the next...' He dropped down onto the bed and rubbed his temple with his free hand. 'It was supposed to be convenient. Fun.'

'Love is anything *but* convenient,' Scott said sagely.

'I didn't say I loved her.'

'Didn't need to. Why else would you be hiding out?'

Scott had a point. He'd run like a scared little kid, tail between his legs, all because she'd drawn the line at sex. In what universe would he be upset by *that*? It was guilt-free—for once *he* didn't have to be the bad guy.

'I don't know if I love her.'

'Are you feeling miserable?'

'Yes.'

'Miserable' was probably a few notches down from the aching in his chest that had appeared when he'd sailed out of Newcastle that morning.

'Confused?'

'Hell, yeah.'

'Lost?' Scott didn't bother waiting for an answer. 'That's what love feels like.'

'It blows.'

Scott laughed. 'It only blows before you sort things out. Then it's pretty bloody amazing. Kinda funny how the tables have turned.'

'I'm not laughing.'

He wanted to throw something—anything that might help him release some of the deadening weight in his limbs.

'So what's your plan of attack?'

'Plan?'

'To get Chantal back. Jeez—keep up, Brodie.'

And there was the rub. 'It's hard to get someone back if you didn't have them in the first place.'

'Did you tell her how you felt?' Scott sounded as though he were explaining something to a dumb animal for the tenth time.

'Well, no.'

'Did you even try?'

Brodie groaned inwardly, this was *way* out of his comfort zone. He was used to being the one giving advice—as he'd done with Scott not that long ago. Why couldn't he seem to sort out his own situation?

'I kind of went a little...caveman.'

'Wow—and you're wondering why she didn't give you anything?'

'She didn't want it. I could tell.' He remembered the look in her eyes, almost as if she was pleading with him to leave.

'She's got a thing about being independent—you can't change that.' Scott sighed. 'She needs her space.'

'I know.'

He rubbed a hand over his face. Of course she wanted to be her own person, but that didn't stop him wanting to protect her. Was it completely hopeless?

'How did I screw it up so bad?'

'Is she worth the pain?'

'Yes.'

The word slipped out before he'd even had time to weigh up possible answers. Uttering that one little word had released the tension from his neck and lifted the heaviness from his shoulders. Was it possible that he was in *love* with Chantal Turner?

'What should I do?'

'Aren't *you* supposed to be the lady whisperer?' Scott teased.

'I'm lost, man. She makes me question everything and I've got no clue what to do next.'

'What do you do when you wipe out?'

Brodie smiled—he could always count on Scott to put something in *his* terms. 'Are you trying to tell me I need to give it another go?'

'I'm not trying to tell you—I *am* telling you. I know Chantal is tough. You need to let her know how you feel— she's not great with ambiguity.'

'What do I say?'

'You'll figure it out. But I would start with an apology. There's no excuse for going caveman.'

Brodie put the phone down and stared at it long and hard. He would figure it out... But having Chantal meant sacrificing other things. To be with her he would need to be away from his family more. He couldn't expect her to drop her dreams of being a dancer and move to Queensland with him.

If this thing between him and Chantal was going to work then other things needed to change too.

He reached for the phone and sucked in a huge breath, dialling his father's number quickly, before he could change his mind.

CHAPTER THIRTEEN

HIGHWAY SCENERY BLURRED past as Sydney faded away in Chantal's rearview mirror. Her old car struggled to keep up with the speed limit, but she was moving…and that was all that mattered.

Last night she'd stood tall in the face of criticism from the bar manager, keeping her head high and knowing that she would make it through to the end of the contract like the professional she was. Knowing that, no matter how dire her situation, she was supporting herself.

Thoughts of Brodie were insistent, but she cranked up the music to drown them out.

After spending the morning at her audition for the Harbour Dance Company she'd gone looking for a cheap apartment to rent. Luck must have been on her side. A tiny one-bedroom place had been vacant for a few weeks and the owner was desperate to get someone in. As she'd signed the paperwork a call had come from the dance company, congratulating her on a successful audition.

Now she was on her way to visit her mother and collect all the boxes she'd stored there. Everything had turned out the way she'd wanted it to—once her bar contract was over it would all be perfect. So why didn't she have a sense of accomplishment and relief?

Brodie.

He'd been the only thing on her mind since she'd walked

away. It had barely been three days and already there was a gaping hole in her life where he'd inserted himself in their short time together. She missed his cheeky smile, the way his arms felt as they squeezed her against him, his lips. The unmanageable desire that materialised whenever he was around. How could she have let herself fall so hard? So quickly and so deeply?

Her childhood home came into view as Chantal rounded the corner at Beach Road, where blue water lined the quiet coast of Batemans Bay. *Home sweet home.*

The roads were empty. Most of the tourists from Canberra would have gone home by now. Work would be slow for her mum…the motels and self-contained units that dotted the shoreline wouldn't need extra cleaning services now that summer was over. Hopefully she still had a gig with the local high school to at least cover rent and bills. Though there would be little left over after the essentials were covered.

Chantal pulled into the parking bay of the apartment block and killed the engine. Stepping out of the car, she smiled at the way the number on their letterbox still hung at a funny angle and the squat garden gnome she'd given her mother one Christmas still guarded the steps up to their second-floor apartment.

The stairs were rickety beneath her feet, and the railing's paintwork peeled off in rough chunks. She was certain it had been white at one point—now it looked closer to the colour of pale custard. The doorbell trilled and footsteps immediately sounded from within the front room. Her mother appeared and ushered Chantal inside with brisk familiarity.

'You should have called. I would have put afternoon tea on.' Her mother enveloped her in a quick hug.

Frances Turner's affection was like everything else she did: quick, efficient and with minimal fuss. She'd never been overly demonstrative while Chantal was growing up, but age had softened her edges.

'No need,' Chantal said, smiling and waving her hand. 'I'm here to visit you—not to eat.'

It was more that she hadn't wanted her mother to feel obligated to go out and buy biscuits, or the fancy tea she liked to drink when Chantal came over. It was easy to see where her desire to keep up appearances had come from.

'Sit, sit...'

Frances gestured to the couch—a tattered floral two-seater that had yellowed with age. Chantal remembered using the back of it as a substitute *barre* while practising for her ballet exams.

'How are you?'

'I'm good.' She smiled brightly, pulling her lips up into a curve and hoping her mother didn't look too closely. 'I got a call this morning. I'm joining the Harbour Dance Company.'

Frances clapped her hands together. 'I *knew* you could do it, baby girl.'

'Thanks, Mum.'

'Why the sad face?' Frances studied her with olive-green eyes identical to hers. Nothing got past those eyes. 'What's going on?'

'Oh, it's nothing,' Chantal said, but she couldn't force the tremble from her voice. 'Boy problems.'

'Derek's not giving you trouble again, is he?' Her thin lips pulled into a flat line. Her mother had hated Derek from day one—something Chantal should have paid more attention to.

'No, Derek is long gone.' She rolled her eyes. 'I've been spending some time with an old friend. It got...confusing.'

'How so?' Frances motioned for Chantal to follow her into the kitchen.

Yellow floral linoleum covered the floor, matching the

painted yellow dining chairs and the small round dining table. The kitchen was her favourite part of the unit— it was kind of garish and dated, but it had the heart of a good home.

She traced her fingertip along the length of a photo on the wall. Chantal stood with her mother, wearing a jazz dance costume they'd stayed up till midnight sequinning the night before a competition. She had a gap-toothed grin and her mother looked exhausted. She didn't remember her mother looking that way at the time. All she'd cared about was the trophy clutched in her young hand.

Guilt scythed through her.

'He doesn't get me and I don't get him. We're different people.'

'But you liked him enough to spend time with him?' Frances twisted the tap, holding the kettle under the running water with her other hand.

'I did.' *I do*...

'And you think it's not good to be different?' Her mother threw her a look she'd seen a lot growing up. She called it the *Get off your high horse* look.

'It's not that. It's just...' How could she explain it? 'He wanted to do everything for me. And I'm capable of doing things myself. I *want* to do things myself. I don't need some knight in shining armour to rescue me.'

Her mother would be the one person who would understand. She'd stood on her own two feet since Chantal's father had walked out. She knew what it meant to be independent—what it meant to achieve things on your own.

'And that bothers you?'

'It does. It's like he can't understand that I need to fix my own problems.' She sighed. 'I want to be able to say that I made my way without any hand-outs.'

'Accepting help is not the same as accepting a handout, Chantal. There's no gold medal for struggling through life on your own.'

The kettle whistled, cutting into their conversation with a loud screech. Frances lifted it from the stove and poured the piping hot water into two mugs with pictures of cats all over them.

'I know that.'

'Don't you think I would have accepted some help if it was available when you were growing up?'

The question rattled Chantal. 'But you used to tell me that it was us against the world and we had to work hard.'

'I wanted you to be strong, baby girl. I wanted you to be tough.' She dropped the teabags into the bin and handed a mug to Chantal. 'Sometimes being strong means knowing when you can't do it on your own. Accepting help doesn't make you weak.'

They moved to the table, and Chantal was glad to be sitting on something solid. Her knees had turned to jelly, and her breath was escaping her lungs in a long whoosh. Her mother had tipped all her long-held beliefs on their head.

'I would have *killed* for someone to come along and offer a hand when you were younger.' Frances blew on the curling steam from the tea. 'Though I feel like I did a pretty good job with you, considering.'

A smile tugged at the corners of Chantal's lips. 'Would it be conceited if I agree?'

'Not at all.' Frances reached across the small table and patted the back of her hand.

'I've stuffed up, haven't I?'

Realisation flooded her, running across her nerves until her whole body was alight with the knowledge that she'd thrown away something important. Something special.

Brodie.

She didn't want to have him back in her life. She didn't want to love him.

But she did.

She'd known it was more than sex from the first time she'd woken up in his arms. But it hadn't been until she'd stood at the edge of his boat, with the freedom of the open waters dancing in her hair, looking down at the dolphins, that she'd realised how much he would do for her. That he wanted to show her what she was missing out on by being so narrow-minded.

And what had she done to return the favour? She'd picked a fight with him…refused to let him in. She'd told him to go. No matter how much time passed, she'd never forget the hurt written on his face when she'd told him not to come after her.

How could she possibly fix it?

'Nothing is irreversible, baby girl.'

Could she let herself believe that? Would she be able to handle the rejection if the damage was too much? Funny how a few weeks ago the thought of another dance company rejecting her had been her driving force. Now her victory seemed hollow without Brodie in her life. She loved dance—it was in her blood—but a world without him seemed…hopeless. Grey.

'I need to get my stuff. I've got an apartment in Sydney now.' Her voice was hollow, her movements stiff and jerky, as if she were being directed by puppet strings.

'Go to him, Chantal. The stuff can wait. *Things* can wait.' Frances stood and gave Chantal a gentle shove towards the front door. 'He might not.'

'I don't know how to get to him.' There were too many variables…too many things to deal with. What if he'd already left for Queensland?

'Find a way—you always do.'

Chantal surprised her mother by pulling her in for a big hug—a *real* hug. Planting a kiss on her cheek, she grabbed her bag and headed for the front door. Canberra airport was the closest airport that would allow her to fly to Brisbane, but it was a two-hour drive away. She didn't even know the name of his company.

Her sneakers hit the steps in quick succession and didn't slow as she raced towards her car.

'Call me when you find him!' Frances called out.

'I will.'

She slammed the door too hard in her haste, the sound ringing out like a shot. Was she *doing* this?

Chantal bit down on her lip and looked at her mobile phone in its holder on the inside of her windscreen. There was one person who could help her. She had no idea if his number was still the same, or if he would protect Brodie rather than talk to her. But she had to try.

As she paused for a red light Chantal tapped the screen and dialled a number.

'Hello?' Scott's voice echoed through the car.

'Scott, it's Chantal. I'm hoping you can help me…'

Brodie stood in the helm, staring blankly out at the harbour. The moored boats were lined up in tidy rows, the *Princess 56* blending into the Sydney scene better than it had in Newcastle. He couldn't be anywhere on the boat without remembering Chantal.

Was she back in the city by now? Doubt rooted him to the deck. Not because he didn't believe in his feelings for her, but because he had no idea if she would ever reciprocate. He couldn't remember a time when a girl had left him so strung out…except for the Weeping Reef situation with Chantal the first time around.

Chantal: two. Brodie: zero.

Giggling came from a couple walking past the boat— the sound of two people in love. He looked away, focusing on the dials in the cockpit. He knew he should sail home, but something had stopped him from preparing the yacht.

The beautiful views and the freedom of sailing felt wasted without Chantal. No matter how opulent the scenery, it was marked by her absence.

He turned his phone over in his hands. He could call her, invite her for a drink. Apologise for pushing too hard. Then what?

Those three little words hung over him like a dead weight. Three. Little. Words.

They changed everything. He'd never loved any woman before—he hadn't thought he had any love left over after his family had taken their share. But she seemed to pull emotion from him that he'd never even known existed. It had forced him to do things he'd never thought he could... like confront his father.

The *Princess 56* was waiting for him, ready and willing. It sat there patiently, needing him only to make a decision. He could either find out where Chantal was or he could sail home.

No, he wasn't going home without her.

Scott was right—he *had* to try again. He *had* to be sure there wasn't a chance for them. His attraction to her had always been more than he'd admitted. More than her gorgeous legs, her dancing, the sex. It was something so frighteningly intense and real that he'd been unable to process it until it was too late.

Brodie was about to pick up his phone to dial her number when it buzzed. Lydia's smiling face flashed up on the screen.

'Hey, Lyds.'

'Hey, Brodie.' There was hesitation in his sister's voice. 'So...Dad called.'

'He did?' Something lifted in Brodie's chest. His father had ended their call earlier with a promise to get in touch with the girls more often, though Brodie still had his doubts. 'What did he say?'

'He's coming to visit,' Lydia replied. 'Well, he *says* that, but we'll see.'

'Would you *like* him to visit?'

'Yeah, I guess.' She hesitated. 'It would be good to see him.'

He sincerely hoped his father lived up to his promise. He'd got a sense that his father's attitude had changed—there'd seemed to be something more receptive about him that had been lacking in the past. Something down in his gut told him that their conversation had been a shifting point for the older man—a reality check that his family needed him. That his daughters needed him.

Brodie could get by on his own, but he had plans to make Chantal a part of his life more permanently—and that meant he couldn't always play the role of pseudo father. The girls needed to know they could rely on their real father as well. Hopefully this was the beginning of all that.

Lydia caught his attention by launching into a new problem—something to do with Ellen and how she was trying to mother her, even though she was the youngest sibling. But Brodie was no longer listening.

A figure hovered nearby on the jetty. Long legs, long dark hair.

Chantal.

'Brodie, are you listening to me?'

Lydia's indignant tone brought his attention back to the call. 'Sorry, Lyds. I have to go.'

He stepped out onto the upper deck and tried to get a better look at the figure. Was it really her?

'But I need your *help.*' His sister sounded as though she were about to cry. 'That's *why* I called you.'

'I'll help you. But I need to do something for me first.'

She sniffled. 'What's more important than talking to your sister?'

He jogged over to the stairs, taking them as quickly as his legs would allow. 'Love.'

'Is this about that girl?' Lydia asked, her voice returning to normal.

'It is.'

'You *love* her?'

'I do, Lyds. I'm going to ask her if she loves me back.'

'Dibs on being the maid of honour,' Lydia said. 'Call me later. Tell me *everything.*'

'I promise.'

Brodie rushed to the jetty and looked around. Late afternoon had given way to early evening and the sun was lowering itself into the water along the horizon. Autumn had started weeks ago but it had only now taken on its first chill of the year, and the cool air prickled his exposed forearms.

People milled about, stopping to take photos of the yachts. Dodging a father towing two small children, Brodie jogged to where he'd seen the figure standing. He couldn't locate Chantal amongst the swarming tourist crowd.

The girl with dark hair had disappeared—had it even been her?

He walked up past the yacht club entrance, past the other boats, until he neared the hotel that sprawled along the water's edge.

He was going crazy. His imagination was playing him for a fool. Why would she come to him when he'd stuffed things up? He hadn't even been able to tell her that he loved her. She deserved better than that.

He headed back to the boat, turning his phone over in his hands. His thumb hovered over the unlock button, ready to dial her number. As he walked across the boarding ramp and raked a hand through his hair he stopped to rub the tense muscles in his neck.

'Brodie?'

Chantal walked out from the cabin, hands knotted in front of her. Long dark strands tumbled around her shoulders, the messy waves scattered by the gentle breeze. A skirt with blue and green shades bleeding into one another swirled around her ankles with each step. A long gold chain weighted by a blue stone glinted around her neck. She looked like a mermaid…a siren. A fantasy.

'What are you doing here?' he asked, his heart hammering against his ribs.

'I thought you'd gone back to Queensland.'

She bundled her hair over one shoulder, toying with the ends as he'd noticed her doing whenever she was anxious. He noticed everything about her now.

'I was supposed to.'

'Why did you stay?'

Light flickered across her face—a ray of hopefulness that dug deep into his chest.

'Unfinished business.'

'With who?'

The question emerged so quietly it might have come from his imagination. But her lips had moved; her eyes were burning into his.

'With you, Chantal. Why do you have to make everything so hard?'

A smile tugged at the corner of her lips. 'I'm difficult, I guess.'

'You are.'

He rubbed at the back of his neck, wishing that his body would calm down so he could be in control of the conversation. Instead his central nervous system conspired against him by sending off signals left, right and centre. There was something about the mere presence of her that had him crackling with electricity. Those parts of him had been dead before her.

'I'm sorry I pushed you away.' She drew a deep breath.

'I'm sorry I wouldn't let you help. I've been afraid of letting anyone close—not just after my divorce but for a long time.'

'You do seem to have trouble accepting help...'

What if he didn't accept her apology? It would be her own fault. She'd been stubborn as a bull from day one, determined to keep a wall between her and the outside world. Only now she wanted to tear down anything standing between her and Brodie. She wanted to remove all barriers—even the ones that had been there so long that they had cemented themselves in.

'I'm working on it,' she said solemnly, swallowing against a rising tide of emotion. 'I thought that I needed to do everything on my own because that's what my mother did. I wanted to be strong...to be my own person.'

He rubbed a hand along his jaw. 'It's a lonely way to live.'

'It is.' She nodded. 'I've been so concerned with making everyone think I was leading this successful life that I put no time into my reality. I only cared about my career, and I almost lost the best thing that ever happened to me.'

'Which is...?' His green eyes reached hers, the burning stare making her knees shake and her limbs quiver.

'You, Brodie. You're an amazing friend, and I lost you once because I refused to acknowledge my feelings. I'm not doing it again.'

She stepped towards him, resisting the urge to reach out and flatten her palms against the soft cotton shirt covering his chest.

'I don't want your friendship, Chantal.' He ground the words out, his teeth gritted, jaw tense.

Her breath hitched. The flight response was tugging against her desire to fight. *No!* She'd come too far to turn away—she could make him see how much she cared. She could make him see that she could change. That she *had* changed already, thanks to him.

'You asked me that night if I felt something for you.' Memories flickered: the sensation of dancing in his arms. The scents. The heat. The intoxicating attraction. 'I never had the chance to answer and then you were gone. I spent eight years convincing myself I'd made an error of judgment. I'd got caught up in the emotion. But I *did* feel something.'

'And now?'

'I want you in my life, Brodie. I want to sail away with you. I *want* your friendship, but I want more than that too.' She squeezed her eyes closed for a moment so she would have the courage to speak again. 'I love you.'

In the silence of waiting for his reaction she'd never felt so vulnerable in her life. No matter how many stages she'd performed on, no matter how much rejection she'd faced before—this was it. She was at a turning point, at the edge of falling into something wonderful. Her breath caught in her throat.

'I'll protect you even when you don't think you need it—I can't help that.' His voice caught, the scratch edge telling her that he was fighting for control too. 'But I'll support you in being your own person.'

She nodded, her breath caught in her throat.

'I'll help you with everything. I will *always* be there for you.'

She sucked on her lower lip, her mind screaming out for her to touch him. But she didn't want to stop his words, didn't want to risk ruining things with him again. If only he would say those words back to her.

I love you.

'I'll make you part of my crazy needy family.' He reached forward and drew her close. 'But I know now that I don't need to be your knight in shining armour. I pushed too hard at the bar. I understand that you need your independence. So I propose that we be our own people... together.'

'Oh, Brodie.' Relief coursed through her, buckling her knees so she sagged against him. The warmth of his body relaxed her, calmed her.

'As much as I love my family, I want to be my own person too. You made me see that. I'm going to put my own needs first for a change—and that starts with loving you.'

She looked up at him, catching his mouth as it came down to hers. The taste of him sent her senses into a spin, the gentle pressure of his lips making her feel as if she'd come home. His tongue met with hers, all the relief and desire and love exploding within her like New Year's fireworks. This was it—this was how life was meant to be.

She broke away from the kiss. 'What needs might they be?'

'Specific needs,' he whispered against her ear, his warm breath sending a shiver down her spine. 'Needs that can only be met by stubborn brunette dancers who like to practise yoga.'

'I might know someone who fits the bill.' She ran her hand under his T-shirt and pressed against the hard muscles in his stomach, as if memorising every ridge and detail of him. 'But she's pretty busy these days. I heard a rumour that she finally made it into a dance company.'

His eyes lit up and he hoisted her up in the air. 'You did?'

The harbour lights blurred as he spun them around. The sky darkened as each moment passed. Somehow it felt as though the universe was cementing their decision to be together.

'I did.' She laughed as he brought her back down. Solid ground would never feel the same again.

'I never had any doubts.'

'You were the only one.' She shot him a rueful smile.

'Not true.' He cupped her face with his hands and pressed another exploratory kiss to her lips. 'But you *do* need a little help with the constant doubt.'

'Are you testing me?'

'Maybe.' A sly smile pulled at his lips.

'Well, I accept your help.' She jabbed a finger into the centre of his chest, unable to conceal a grin. 'So there.'

'Chantal, I need to be able to help you. I need to be part of your life in a way that no one else can. I'll give you everything you deserve. I'll do everything I can to give you the life you want.'

The thumping of his heart reverberated against her ear.

'I'm going to run the business from Sydney.'

'Can you do that?' Her head jerked up.

'That's the best bit about being the boss.' He grinned. 'I can do whatever I like.'

'But what about your family?'

'I put a call in to my father. He's going to start sharing the load with me.' A flash of vulnerability streaked across Brodie's eyes. ''Bout time.'

'Really? That's wonderful.'

'Besides, Queensland is only a state away, and I'm sure you'll need a break at some point. I'll have to split my time across the two states but I know I can manage it.' He chuckled. 'Besides, the girls will be desperate to meet you.'

'I'd love to meet *them*. I never had what you had growing up. I know your family isn't perfect, but I've never been part of a family like that before.'

The idea was frightening—what if his sisters hated her?

'They'll love you. I know it.' He stroked her hair, pressing his lips to her forehead. 'But you were right to point out that I hide behind my family responsibilities. I *have* been hiding.'

She smiled against his chest. 'You can't hide any more.'

'I don't want to. I love you, Chantal.'

He spoke into her hair, his arms tight around her shoulders, his hand caressing her back.

Music wafted over the night air from the boat next to them.

Brodie wrapped his arms around her waist, moving her to the music. 'And I always said pretty girls shouldn't have to dance on their own.'

'I won't dance on my own ever again.'

* * * * *

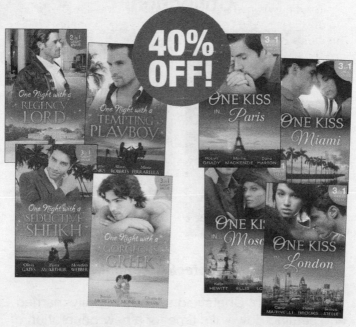

MILLS & BOON®

Two superb collections!

40% OFF!

Would you rather spend the night with a seductive sheikh or be whisked away to a tropical Hawaiian island? Well, now you don't have to choose! Get your hands on both collections today and get 40% off the RRP!

Hurry, order yours today at
www.millsandboon.co.uk/TheOneCollection

0215_INSHIP1

MILLS & BOON®

The Chatsfield Collection!

2 BOOKS FREE!

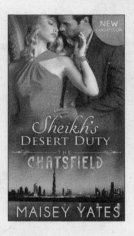

Style, spectacle, scandal...!

With the eight Chatsfield siblings happily married and settling down, it's time for a new generation of Chatsfields to shine, in this brand-new 8-book collection! The prospect of a merger with the Harrington family's boutique hotels will shape the future forever. But who will come out on top?

Find out at
www.millsandboon.co.uk/TheChatsfield2

CHATSFIELD_PROMO_BK

MILLS & BOON®

Classic romances from your favourite authors!

3 in 1 GREAT VALUE

40% OFF!

The Jarrods: Temptation

MAUREEN CHILD TESSA RADLEY KATHIE DENOSKY

By Request

The Australian's Desire

MARION LENNOX LILIAN DARCY

By Request

Royal and Ruthless

ROBYN DONALD ANNIE WEST CHRISTINA HOLLIS

By Request

Whether you love tycoon billionaires, rugged ranchers or dashing doctors, this collection has something to suit everyone this New Year. Plus, we're giving you a huge 40% off the RRP!

Hurry, order yours today at
www.millsandboon.co.uk/NYCollection

0215_INSHIP2

MILLS & BOON®

Seven Sexy Sins!

CATHY WILLIAMS
To Sin with the Tycoon

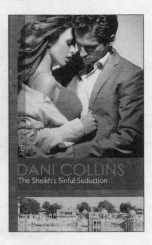

DANI COLLINS
The Sheikh's Sinful Seduction

The true taste of temptation!

From greed to gluttony, lust to envy, these fabulous
stories explore what seven sexy sins mean in
the twenty-first century!

Whether pride goes before a fall, or wrath leads to a
passion that consumes entirely, one thing is certain:
the road to true love has never been more enticing.

Collect all seven at
www.millsandboon.co.uk/SexySins

0315_ST_9

MILLS & BOON®

MODERN™

POWER, PASSION AND IRRESISTIBLE TEMPTATION

A sneak peek at next month's titles...

In stores from 20th March 2015:

- **The Billionaire's Bridal Bargain** – Lynne Graham
- **Carrying the Greek's Heir** – Sharon Kendrick
- **His Diamond of Convenience** – Maisey Yates
- **The Italian's Deal for I Do** – Jennifer Hayward

In stores from 3rd April 2015:

- **At the Brazilian's Command** – Susan Stephens
- **The Sheikh's Princess Bride** – Annie West
- **Olivero's Outrageous Proposal** – Kate Walker
- **The Hotel Magnate's Demand** – Jennifer Rae

Available at WHSmith, Tesco, Asda, Eason, Amazon and Apple

Just can't wait?
Buy our books online a month before they hit the shops!
visit www.millsandboon.co.uk

These books are also available in eBook format!

0315/01